ICING IVY

A Jane Stuart and Winky Mystery

ICING
IVY

EVAN MARSHALL

Thorndike Press • Chivers Press
Waterville, Maine USA Bath, England

This Large Print edition is published by Thorndike Press®, USA and by Chivers Press, England.

Published in 2003 in the U.S. by arrangement with Kensington Books, an imprint of Kensington Publishing Corp.

Published in 2003 in the U.K. by arrangement with the author.

U.S. Softcover 0-7862-5388-6 (Paperback Series)
U.K. Hardcover 0-7540-7234-7 (Chivers Large Print)
U.K. Softcover 0-7540-7235-5 (Camden Large Print)

The text of this Large Print edition is unabridged.
Other aspects of the book may vary from the original edition.

Set in 16 pt. Plantin by Myrna S. Raven.

Printed in the United States on permanent paper.

British Library Cataloguing-in-Publication Data available

Library of Congress Cataloging-in-Publication Data

Marshall, Evan, 1956–
    Icing Ivy / Evan Marshall.
      p. cm.
    ISBN 0-7862-5388-6 (lg. print : sc : alk. paper)
    1. Stuart, Jane (Fictitious character) — Fiction. 2. Winky (Fictitious character) — Fiction. 3. Women cat owners — Fiction. 4. Literary agents — Fiction. 5. Cats — Fiction. 6. Large type books. I. Title.
PS3563.A72236I27 2003
  813'.54—dc21   2003042657

To my mother,
Maxine Marshall,
with love

Let justice be done, though the heavens fall.
— Legal maxim

Acknowledgments

I would like to express my thanks and appreciation to the following people:

Frank Corso, Joseph M. Holtzman, Ph.D., and Warren Marshall for telling me about Trotsky and the ice pick. Or was it an ice ax . . . ?

John Baglieri, personal trainer extraordinaire, for lending me his name.

Ellen Reichert, for telling me about superfecundation.

Florence Phillip, for telling me about the cascadura.

John Scognamiglio, my editor, for his wisdom and encouragement.

Maureen Walters, for being the best agent an agent could ask for.

My family and friends, for their love and support.

MT. MUNSEE LODGE

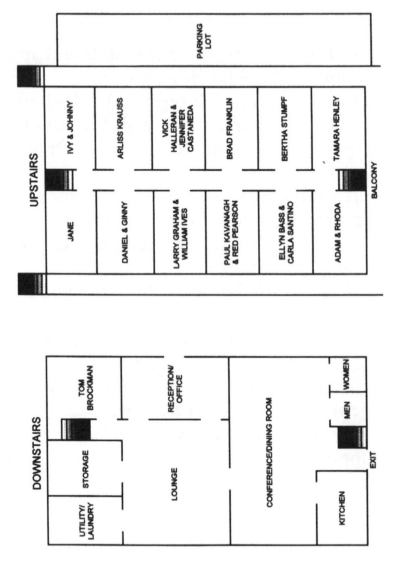

UPSTAIRS

PARKING LOT

BALCONY

IVY & JOHNNY
JANE

ARLISS KRAUSS
DANIEL & GINNY

VICK HALLERAN & JENNIFER CASTANEDA
LARRY GRAHAM & WILLIAM IVES

BRAD FRANKLIN
PAUL KAVANAGH & RED PEARSON

BERTHA STUMPF
ELLYN BASS & CARLA SANTINO

TAMARA HENLEY
ADAM & RHODA

DOWNSTAIRS

TOM BROCKMAN

STORAGE

UTILITY/ LAUNDRY

RECEPTION/ OFFICE

LOUNGE

CONFERENCE/DINING ROOM

WOMEN

MEN

KITCHEN

EXIT

Chapter One

"Back soon," Jane called to Daniel, who smiled and waved from the office doorway. Then she turned and ran across Center Street onto the village green. Stanley, who had preceded Jane by less than a minute, was nowhere in sight.

She giggled. He must be hiding. A silly thrill building inside her, she started down one of the paths that transected the green, walking slowly and peering behind the trunks of the massive oaks that rose from the snow. "I know you're here somewhere."

But there was only silence, broken occasionally by the whoosh of cars passing on Packer Road, far to her right.

The ornate white Victorian bandstand came into view. Could Stanley be hiding in there? She squinted but saw no one.

Wham. Something hit the back of her coat, hit hard. "Ow." She spun around, not liking this game anymore. Stanley was laughing, his sand-colored hair blowing in the chill wind. Clapping his gloved hands together, he ran toward her, his camel coat hanging loose and open on his broad shoulders. When he saw her face, his smile vanished. "Sorry. Did that hurt you?"

"Yes," she said petulantly. "You didn't have to throw it so hard."

"I'm sorry." He put his hand on her shoulder and turned her toward him. His dark brown eyes were tearing in the cold. He kissed her on the lips. "Forgive me?"

She regarded him for a moment. Such a sweet man, so often like a boy. "Yes," she said at last. "Fine behavior for a police detective."

"Excuse me," he said with a disbelieving laugh. "You're the one who said she loved snowball fights at Christmas."

"True. I just don't like to be the one getting hit."

He shook his head. "Not exactly the kind of behavior one would expect from Shady Hills' own literary agent, either."

"I think this town knows me better than that." With a grin, she took his arm and cuddled against him, and they began to walk.

They were nearing the other side of the green, where Center Street continued in its U shape. Across the street, the window of Whipped Cream, the café where they planned to have lunch, twinkled red and green and blue. Ginny always insisted on colored lights, dismissing with a laugh the opinion of many Shady Hills residents that white lights were more appropriate for the upscale village.

"Pretty, isn't it?" Jane said as a black Mercedes passed in front of them and drove slowly around the green. She scanned the line of mock-Tudor shops that ran around Center Street — half-timbered, with steeply pitched roofs and a profusion of gables. With their coating of snow, they looked like something out of a fairy tale. "I do love this town."

From behind them came the sound of car brakes suddenly applied. Jane and Stanley turned. The black Mercedes had stopped in front of Jane's office, and now a man and a woman got out. From this distance, Jane couldn't tell if she knew them.

"Probably out-of-town shoppers," Stanley said, and they turned again toward lunch.

"Jane. Jane, is that you?"

It was a voice Jane had thought she'd never hear again.

Jane spun around. The woman who had gotten out of the car was waving broadly.

Jane squinted. Could it be? She drew in her breath sharply.

"Who is it?" Stanley asked.

11

A violent shiver ran through her. "It's Ivy," she said in a marveling tone. "Ivy Benson. You remember, Marlene's mother."

"Ivy Benson?" He looked shocked. "But I thought you two — I mean, didn't she —"

"Not want to be friends anymore?" she finished for him. "That's right. At least, that's what she said."

And Jane couldn't blame Ivy. A little over two years before, Ivy's daughter, Marlene, had come east to work as nanny to Jane's son, Nicholas — and wound up dead. Though Marlene had brought about her own demise by means of a chain of lies and deceptions, Ivy had blamed Jane for Marlene's death. And a friendship that had begun when the two women were college roommates had ended. At least, Jane had thought it had.

Ivy was running along the path toward Jane, waving frantically. As she approached, Jane could see that this was indeed the same old Ivy, compact but curvaceous, a thick mop of tightly waved blond hair crowning a round, sweet face with huge blue eyes. Even in her amazement at seeing Ivy, Jane couldn't help noticing that her old friend was looking exceptionally well. What had appeared to be her usual mass of hair was actually an artful cut, her once-untended brows appeared to have been professionally tamed, and the simple gold drop earrings and belted black cashmere coat were definitely several steps up from the old Kmart stuff that had once been her trademark.

Ivy, quick-stepping toward Jane in her high heels, was crying, and Jane found herself crying too as she welcomed Ivy into her arms.

"Ivy Benson," she said at last, drawing back. "What are you doing here?"

Ivy wiped away her tears with a black-gloved hand. "I was worried you wouldn't want to see me again. After what I said to you when . . . after what I said. But you're my best friend, Jane. I never felt right after what happened. And now that I'm living in New York —"

"You're living in New York?" Jane asked, incredulous. "Ivy Benson, who said she'd never leave Detroit?"

Ivy shrugged. "People change," she said brightly. "You wouldn't be*lieve* how I've changed. I've got my own *fabulous* apartment, a great job working for a newspaper, and . . ." She turned toward the man who had gotten out of the car and who was now strolling up the path. Jane turned to look at him, too, and found herself gaping. Good heavens, this man, whoever he was, was handsome. He was of medium height, lean, with an abundance of wavy black hair around a strong-boned face with refined, aristocratic features. He looked about thirty-five, vital and youthful against Ivy's forty. He reminded Jane of an updated Tyrone Power.

"Jane," Ivy said formally, gesturing for the man to come over, "I'd like you to meet my *boyfriend*" — she placed special emphasis on the word — "John Baglieri."

John came forward and took Jane's hand, his lips parting in a beautiful white-toothed smile. "Pleasure. Call me Johnny." There was nothing refined about the way he spoke, which was with an accent — Brooklyn? The Bronx? Jane couldn't be sure. It was what she would have called a New York "street" accent.

Stanley approached them, smiling politely.

"And this," Jane said, "is *my* boyfriend, Stanley Greenberg."

Stanley shook their hands enthusiastically. "I believe we've met, Mrs. Benson. At the police station, after your daughter . . ."

Ivy's face darkened. "Yes, of course we have."

14

"So," Jane said, eager to change the subject. "Ivy, you still haven't told me what you're doing here."

"Like I said, I've missed you, Jane. There I was in New York City — what, twenty-five miles away? — and you and I weren't even speaking. It was killing me. So I said to Johnny, 'Hey. It's four days before Christmas. I've got the day off. Let's go see Jane. Surprise her. If she won't see me, I'll understand, but at least I'll have tried.' So here we are. Johnny and I thought we'd take you to lunch." Ivy shot a quick glance at Stanley. "Both of you, of course."

"Actually, we were just on our way to have lunch," Stanley said, indicating Whipped Cream.

"Perfect," Ivy cried in a high squeak, and they all crossed the street and entered the shop. Jane's friend Ginny, Whipped Cream's only server, was clearing a table when they entered. With a curious smile she approached the small group, and Jane introduced Ivy and Johnny to her. Then they settled at a table near the café's great crackling fireplace.

"I can't believe it," Ivy said to herself as she perused her menu. "Here I am with my old friend Jane." She wiped a tear from

15

her eye. "Can't believe it."

Jane watched her old friend. Hair, brows, jewelry, and clothing notwithstanding, she hadn't changed, not really. Though pretty, she still had a cheap edge to her, an indefinable . . . flooziness.

Ivy, who hadn't removed her coat, now let it slip from her shoulders to reveal a summer-weight ivory cotton blouse. She shivered, folding her arms and rubbing her upper arms for warmth. "Cold in here."

Inwardly Jane laughed. Ivy never dressed warmly enough.

"Would you like to sit here by the fire?" Stanley asked.

"Nah, thanks, Stan, I'm fine." Ivy gave Jane a fond look. "As Jane'll tell ya, I'm always cold." She opened her bag, stopped, and looked quickly around the table. "Is it okay to smoke in here?"

Ginny approached the table. "Forgive me for eavesdropping, but Charlie and George — they're the owners — don't allow smoking in here."

"Not a prob," Ivy cried, hands raised, then snapped her bag shut. Johnny was shaking his head. Jane's gaze was drawn to his white shirt, tight enough to reveal strong, smooth musculature. A few dark hairs curled at his open collar.

16

As if sensing her gaze, he looked up suddenly, and Jane felt herself blush. "So, Jane," he said, setting aside his menu, "Ivy was trying to explain what it is you do, but I still don't get it. Why don't you explain it to me?"

"Oh, Johnny," Ivy cooed.

"Of course," Jane said. "I'm a literary agent. I represent writers, sell their books to publishers, negotiate their contracts, manage their careers."

"I get it," Johnny said. He shot Ivy a look, as if to ask what was so complicated about that. "Pretty simple, really. And — if you don't mind my asking — does that make a nice living for you?"

Stanley looked up from his menu in surprise.

"I can't complain," Jane replied smoothly.

"What do you do, take a piece of the action?" Johnny asked.

Jane couldn't help making a little frown. Ivy saw it and nudged Johnny. "That's kind of *per*sonal . . ."

"Okay, sorry. Sorry, Jane." Johnny held up his hands.

Jane said, "No problem, I don't mind. I'm on commission, actually, so yes, I guess you could say I take a piece of the

17

action. I've never quite thought of it that way." Laughing breezily, she turned to Stanley, who was not laughing at all, not even smiling, but watching Johnny in a most disconcerting way.

"Stanley," Jane said, a bit too loudly, and he snapped out of his stare. "Why don't you tell Ivy and Johnny what it is you do?"

"Sure," Stanley said, forcing a small smile, "sure. I'm a police detective. Right here in town. Shady Hills Police Department."

For the merest fraction of a second, Johnny's eyes widened. Then he appeared to collect himself. His mouth turned up at the corners, though Jane wouldn't have called it a smile exactly. "Now *that* must be interesting work," Johnny said.

Ivy turned to Johnny with a frown. "You knew that's what he does. He just said he met me after the whole thing with Marlene."

"Sure, right," Johnny said absently, and occupied himself once again with his menu.

"What about you, Johnny?" Jane said. "What kind of work do you do?"

"Huh? Me?" Johnny looked up with a blank expression, as if he'd never been part of the conversation. "I guess you could say

I've got my irons in many fires. Kind of a jack of all trades."

"I see," Jane said, though she didn't see at all. She looked at Stanley. He was staring again.

Mercifully, Ginny appeared. "May I tell you about our specials?"

"Yes, please," Jane said, looking up attentively.

"*Definitely*," Ivy said, "and bring us some rolls or something when you get a chance, would you, hon? I swear I could eat a cow."

"Was that Ivy Benson?" Daniel asked, the minute Jane and Stanley entered the office. Sitting at his desk in the reception room, he had spun away from his computer, amazement on his handsome brown face.

"The one and only." Jane hung her coat in the closet, then took Stanley's.

"What did she want?"

"To see me again." They had exchanged phone numbers.

"Why?"

Jane frowned. "Because she's my oldest friend. She wanted to see me again. I think it was very brave of her."

Daniel shook his head and nibbled

19

thoughtfully on the inside of his lower lip. "She wants something."

"Why do you say that?" Jane asked, finding herself becoming upset.

"Don't you remember the things she said to you? She *blamed* you for Marlene's death, when in truth —"

"I know what happened. You don't have to remind me, believe me." Jane shrugged. "As Ivy herself said, people change. She wants to be friends again. It was good to see her." She turned to Stanley, who sat in Daniel's visitor's chair, lost in thought. "All right, out with it."

Stanley looked up as if startled. "Hm? I was just thinking about that young fellow, Johnny. Bad news, if you ask me."

"Why?" Jane demanded, exasperated. "What is *with* you two?"

Stanley put up his hands defensively. "I could be wrong. It's just a feeling I got."

"Why, because he's a little rough around the edges?"

"No, it's not that. It was the way he was looking at me after he found out I was a cop. And — I don't know, the way he carries himself. I can just tell, Jane, the same way you can immediately tell a good manuscript from a bad one."

Jane didn't want to hear any of this. She

wanted Ivy to be happy. Years ago, when Jane and Ivy were eighteen years old, freshman roommates in college, Ivy had confided to Jane that all she wanted was a good man and a good life. A man who loved her, asleep on the next lounge chair, while Ivy sipped extra-tall piña coladas served by beach boys in brightly colored shirts. Somewhere hot. With palm trees. That was how Ivy had envisioned the good life.

With a faraway smile, Jane turned to Daniel. "Speaking of bad manuscripts, have you had a chance to look at Bertha Stumpf's revised manuscript of *Shady Lady*?" It had taken every bit of Jane's skills of persuasion to get Bertha, who wrote historical romances under the pseudonym Rhonda Redmond, to revise her manuscript for her editor, Harriet Green at Bantam.

"Sure have," Daniel said lightly. "It still stinks."

"Really? Now what's wrong with it?"

"There's still absolutely no conflict between the hero and heroine. There's no reason why they shouldn't walk hand in hand into the sunset on page ten. Not only that, there's no plot. All they do is have sex."

21

"Sounds good to me," Stanley piped up. Jane gave him an irritated look. "Don't you have some criminals to catch?"

He jumped up. "Well, I certainly know where I'm not wanted."

"Give me a break," Jane said, handing him his coat from the closet.

"I had to leave anyway," Stanley said.

"I know." Jane gave him a kiss as he opened the door to leave.

"Hello," Jane heard him say outside, and a moment later he was showing in Rhoda Kagan and her boyfriend, Adam Forrest. "Later," Stanley told Jane, and left.

Rhoda looked smashing, as always, in black slacks and a brilliant indigo sweater. Huge black Bakelite earrings set off her sleekly cut dark brown hair.

"Hello, darling," she said, exchanging cheek kisses with Jane. "You remember Adam."

"Of course." Jane had last seen Adam at a local party about a month earlier. "How are you, Adam? You're looking well."

Adam, independently wealthy, always looked well — trim and tan and neat. Today he wore tan Dockers and an expensive-looking brown sweater. "Thanks, Jane." He seemed nervous, awkward somehow.

"So what's doing, guys?" Jane asked them. "You Christmas shopping?"

Rhoda shot Adam a look.

"Jane," he said, "Rhoda and I . . . well, *I* need to ask you a favor. . . ."

Chapter Two

Florence's gaze was fixed on Winky, whose pregnant tortoiseshell belly swung from side to side as she padded across the family room and out into the foyer. "So what do you think, missus? Are you going to do it?"

Jane sipped her tea. She had just told Florence what Adam had asked her to do.

Adam had recently bought Mt. Munsee Lodge, located at the top of Mt. Munsee at the northernmost end of Shady Hills. The lodge was a popular spot for hikers and campers, except in the winter, when the lodge's previous owner had shut it down. But Adam had come up with an idea to make money in the off-season. He had been sponsoring five-day "theme retreats" on topics ranging from yoga to investing.

Adam had scheduled a retreat for would-be antiques dealers for the following week — the week between Christmas and New Year's — but had learned that morning that its leader would be unable to appear because his wife was quite ill.

It was Rhoda who had come up with the idea of organizing a fiction writers' retreat to take the place of the antiques one.

Florence said, "Why doesn't he forget about it and enjoy the holidays?" A smile brightened her pretty coffee-colored face. "He doesn't need the money."

"Apparently he does," Jane said. "Or, to put it another way, it would help."

"I see . . ." Florence said thoughtfully. "But how can such a thing possibly be arranged on such short notice?"

"The lodge is small, so we wouldn't need many people. And Adam says he always has one-on-one instruction at these retreats — which is another reason why there can't be too many attendees. He said that if I can round up six instructors besides myself, he'll sign up six attendees from a writers' group here in town."

"What writers' group?"

"The Midnight Writers. I had no idea they even existed."

"Could you 'round up' six instructors?" Florence asked.

"I'm not sure. Probably, if I set my mind to it. I'd call editors, authors, other agents — nah, just editors and authors — and could probably come up with six."

"Don't you want to take the week between Christmas and New Year's off? You do that every year."

"True — which is why I'm available. I've been looking forward to spending the time with Nick, but I really do feel I should help Rhoda and Adam out with this. Besides, I've just had my vacation — I'm not in dire need of a rest." Less than a month earlier, Jane had spent two glorious weeks in Antigua. "And I'll make it up to Nick."

"You may miss the blessed event," Florence said, referring to Winky's imminent delivery. She rose from the sofa and took Jane's teacup. "Dinner in twenty minutes." She walked into the kitchen and stopped to glare at Nick's books and papers strewn all over the table. Jane heard her open the back door. "Master Nicholas," Florence called out into the garage. "Put down the snow shovel and come in here. Your homework is all over the table, and from the looks of it, none of it is done."

"Take it easy, I'm coming," came Nick's voice, followed by a giggle from Florence.

Laughing herself, Jane headed for her study off the living room to start making phone calls. The first would be to Adam, to tell him she'd decided to help him out.

It was a few minutes before nine that evening when Jane put down the phone, having successfully recruited six instructors for the fiction writers' retreat.

The phone rang. It was Ivy.

"I had to tell you how terrific it was to see you again, Jane. I hope we can be friends again, after everything that happened. I mean friends like the old days. I didn't get a chance to say that to you today, but I don't blame you at all for Marlene's death. I miss her terribly — she was all I had — but I know that none of it was your fault."

"Thank you, Ivy, I appreciate your saying that. Of course we can be friends again."

"I'm so glad. There was something else I forgot to ask you today. How is little Nicholas?"

"Not so little anymore — ten and a half years old."

"He can't be. I'd love to see him," Ivy said wistfully.

"I'm sure you will one day soon."

"Mmm. It must be nice for you to have him with you at Christmas. I mean, now that Kenneth is gone." Kenneth, Jane's late husband, had died a little over three years before.

"Yes." Jane felt uneasy. "Will you and Johnny be doing anything special for the holidays?"

"He'll be away. Business trip. He says he can't get out of it. You know how it is." Ivy let out a sigh. "This will be my second Christmas without Marlene. I suppose one day I'll get used to it." There was a long silence on the line.

Alone at Christmas . . .

"Ivy," Jane blurted out, "why don't you spend Christmas out here with us?"

"With you? Why, Jane, what an idea. But I couldn't — I'd be in the way."

"No, you wouldn't. We'd love to have you. You'll get to see Nick, and you'll love Florence — she's Nick's nanny, and a wonderful person."

"If you really think it would be all right . . ."

"Of course I do." Then Jane thought of something. "One thing, though. Right after Christmas — next Wednesday — I've got to go to a retreat I'm helping organize." She told Ivy all about it. "But we'd still be together during the holiday."

"True. Hey, Jane, do you think I could come on your retreat *with* you? I'm taking that week off from work. Wouldn't it be a gas?"

Jane frowned. "I don't think that would be possible, unfortunately."

"Yeah, I'd be in the way, I suppose."

"No, it's not that."

"I could help out," Ivy said eagerly. "Hand out paper and pencils, things like that. I'm very organized, as you know."

Jane had never thought of Ivy as being especially organized. She made no comment as to that. "I've never been to this lodge. I'm not sure there's room."

"I guess you'd have your own room, huh?"

"Yes, I imagine."

"Then we could room together. It would be like the old days at school. Wouldn't it be fun? Just you and me, hanging out in our jammies, eating Cheese Curls? What a way to spend the holidays. No chance I'd be lonely then."

Jane's heart went out to her old friend. How could Adam object if Jane shared her room with Ivy? "I guess it would be all right. . . ."

"You don't sound very sure."

"Yes, I'm sure," Jane said kindly. "I'd love to have you with me at the retreat."

"You and me and Cheese Curls. When should I come out to your house?"

The next day was Saturday. "Why not tomorrow? Then we can have the weekend to catch up, and Monday night is Christmas Eve."

"Perfect. Oh, Jane," Ivy said, tears coming into her voice, "I can't tell you how much I've missed you. I'm glad we're not letting what happened ruin our friendship. You're my oldest friend — my best friend."

Still feeling uneasy, Jane averred that she was glad, too. Then they made plans. Ivy, who had no car, would take a Lakeland bus the next morning from New York City's Port Authority Bus Terminal to Shady Hills. Jane would be waiting for her bus.

Chapter Three

Florence entered the dining room bearing a platter of fish fillets covered with a rich brown sauce. Steam rose from the platter.

"That looks wonderful, Florence," Ivy said, craning her neck as Florence set it down.

Florence beamed. "Thank you. It is my very favorite recipe, from my mother — curried cascadura. I do hope you all like it. When I was growing up, we always had it on Christmas Eve — and many other times too. I had to go to my Afro-Caribbean market in Newark for the fish."

Ivy frowned. "Why'd you have to go all the way to Newark?"

"Because that is the only store that imports cascadura, or cascadoo as we call it back home. This fish is found only in Trinidad." Florence gazed across the dining room, a dreamy look in her eyes. "In my country they say,

Those who eat the cascadura will,
The native legend says,

31

Wheresoever they may wander,
End in Trinidad their days."

Jane, her gazed fixed on Florence, said, "Why, that's lovely."

Nick, seated to Ivy's right, was gently petting Winky, who sat on the empty chair beside him. He stroked the cat's mottled orange-and-brown head but was careful not to touch her enlarged belly. "I've eaten this a zillion times," he declared nonchalantly, and Jane and Florence exchanged a smile.

"Indeed you have, little mister, indeed you have." Florence went back to the kitchen for platters of rice and green beans, which she set down on the table. Then she took up serving utensils. "If you'll pass me your plate," she said, reaching toward Ivy.

The telephone rang.

"Let it ring," Jane said breezily. "We're having dinner."

Ivy drew in a little breath and looked around anxiously.

"What's wrong, Ivy?" Jane asked.

The phone continued to ring.

"Nothing," Ivy replied, moving restlessly in her chair. "It's just that . . . maybe it's Johnny."

"Of course," Jane said. "Where is my head?" She jumped up, hurried into the kitchen, and grabbed the phone.

It was indeed Johnny. "Umm, yeah, is this, uh, Joan?"

"It's Jane," she replied, feeling uncomfortable.

"Right, Jane. Sorry. How's it goin'?"

"Fine, Johnny, and you? Ivy said you're away on business?"

"Well, I was — I mean, I was going to be." He sounded as if he didn't want to discuss this with her. "Is Ivy there?"

"Certainly. One moment."

Jane called Ivy, who hurried in. "Thanks, hon," Ivy said, and waited, apparently not wanting to begin her conversation until Jane had left the kitchen. Jane did and was aware of the door being closed quietly behind her.

Ivy and Johnny's conversation didn't last long. Florence was still serving when Ivy returned to the dining room, an odd, preoccupied look on her face.

"Everything okay?" Jane asked.

"Yes," Ivy replied, smiling an uneasy little smile.

"No, it's not," Jane said with a laugh. "What's going on?"

Ivy picked up her fork and poked at a

33

green bean. "Everything's fine, really. It's just that Johnny doesn't have to go away on business after all."

"Ah," Jane said. "And you want to be with him and are embarrassed to tell me. Ivy, don't worry about it. He's your boyfriend. I completely understand."

When Ivy looked up, her face bore no trace of the relieved smile Jane had expected. She still looked troubled. "Thanks, Jane, but he and I were wondering if maybe" — she winced, as if afraid to say the words — "he could come to your retreat too?"

Jane gave her a puzzled look. "Johnny? Why would *he* want to come?"

"It would be kind of a vacation, you know? It's so pretty here — Johnny kept saying so when we drove out on Friday."

Jane didn't know what to make of this. Ivy had always been a bit pushy, often inappropriate, and Jane's instinct was to simply say no. A fiction writers' retreat was no place for Johnny. Besides, if he came, he and Ivy would need a room of their own, and there probably wasn't one to spare. On the other hand, Jane thought, meeting Ivy's expectant gaze, she didn't know that for sure. She should call Adam and find out. Would it really be such a problem if

Johnny did come? He and Ivy could take walks in the woods, do that sort of thing.

"Tell you what I'll do," Jane said. "Right after dinner, I'll call Adam — he owns the lodge. If he says he's got a room for you and Johnny, I have no objections."

Ivy looked apprehensive. "You think he might not have a room?"

"It's a possibility. I understand the lodge is small."

Ivy thought about this, then nodded. "Okay, thanks, Jane." She pressed her fork down on her cascadura fillet, crushing it. "I hope he says yes. It would be so good for Johnny and me."

Jane watched Ivy. It was suddenly clear to Jane that Johnny's coming to the retreat meant a lot to Ivy, that she saw it as more than just a fun getaway for the two of them. Why? Was their relationship somehow in trouble? Did Ivy hope this time away together would solve this trouble?

Dinner felt somehow strained to Jane, though the food was heavenly and they all talked and laughed. It was as if Ivy couldn't wait for the meal to end so that Jane could call Adam.

To Jane's surprise, Adam did have a

spare room and was only too glad to let Ivy and Johnny have it. "You're doing me a tremendous favor, Jane. How could I say no? The room's on me."

"Thanks, Adam," Jane said, surprised to find herself disappointed by his response. Was it that she'd looked forward to just her and Ivy — jammies and Cheese Curls? Or was it Johnny? Somehow she couldn't imagine him at a writers' retreat. The idea made her uneasy. What would he and Ivy do all day? On further reflection, he hadn't struck Jane as the woods-walking type.

Lost in thought, Jane left her study and went in search of Ivy to tell her the news.

Later that evening, Jane, Ivy, Florence, and Nick sat together in the family room watching TV. Since Christmas vacation had officially begun, Nick was allowed to stay up late and had, in fact, chosen to-night's television viewing, a special Christmas episode of his favorite show, *CyberWarriors*. Jane was utterly bored, and it appeared that Ivy and Florence were as well. Nick sat at the edge of the sofa, jumping up and down every time a CyberWarrior laser-blasted a Vultron.

Jane let her gaze travel around the room. The Christmas tree had turned out especially well. Each year she added a new touch, and this year's was a collection of ornaments in the shape of tiny stacks of antique books wrapped with gold bows. Colored lights that reminded her of the window of Whipped Cream twinkled among the tree's branches. Beneath the tree, in a pleasing jumble, were a goodly number of presents. Jane had even run out the day before and bought something for Ivy — a bottle of Norell perfume, which had always been her favorite.

"Mom, look at this," Nick cried. Jane expected to see some especially exciting scene from *CyberWarriors*, but on the TV screen instead was a newscaster looking solemn.

"Good evening. We interrupt our scheduled broadcast to bring you an update on the bus hijacking . . ."

"What bus hijacking?" Jane said.

"Haven't you heard about this, missus? It's the big story right now."

"Shhh, listen," Ivy said, and they all watched the screen.

That morning, in the city of Paterson, New Jersey, a man described as heavily bearded and carrying a briefcase had boarded a New Jersey Transit bus bound ultimately for New York City. Approxi-

37

mately twenty minutes after boarding, as the bus sped eastward on Route 3, he brandished a gun and threatened to detonate a bomb in his briefcase if he did not receive full cooperation. Holding his gun to the driver's head, he commanded the driver to radio headquarters and relay his demands: a million dollars in unmarked twenty-dollar bills for the release of his hostages — the driver and thirty-one other passengers. This ransom was to be waiting for him at Gate B of Giants Stadium in East Rutherford within an hour.

An hour later, the commandeered bus pulled up at Gate B of the stadium, where police waited with the money. At gunpoint the driver opened the doors, and the money was thrown aboard. The gunman checked the money and, apparently satisfied, released the other passengers but not the driver, whom he ordered to shut the doors and take off. The bus then raced westward on Route 3, onto Route 46, then onto Interstate 80. It left I-80 at Shady Hills and sped north into Lincoln Park, where it finally stopped in a wooded area and the gunman disembarked. The authorities, who were interviewing the driver and the passengers, had as yet found no trace of him.

"Can you believe this?" Ivy said, wide-eyed.

The newscaster continued, "Police are combing the woods in the Lincoln Park/ Shady Hills area for signs of this man. We now return to our regularly scheduled programming."

Once again, colorful CyberWarriors and Vultrons filled the screen.

"A million dollars," Ivy said. "Can you imagine?"

"That poor driver," Jane said. "And all those frightened people. I hope they catch him."

The credits for *CyberWarriors* had begun to roll.

"Well," Florence said, rising from the sofa. "It's time a certain young man got to bed, or else Santa Claus won't come with the rest of the presents."

"Come off it, Flo," Nick said. "There's no Santa Claus, and you know it. Besides, all the presents are there already."

"You never know." Florence grinned widely, eyebrows rising. She looked down at Winky. "And from the look of our little miss here, I think she's ready to give us a few presents anytime now."

Chapter Four

Florence was right. The next day, Christmas Day, Winky gave birth to six kittens. She did so in a nest box that Jane (at the advice of Winky's veterinarian, Dr. Singh) had made for her in a corner of the laundry room by filling the bottom of a cardboard carton with old clean towels.

"A trouble-free birth," Florence, emerging from the laundry room, proclaimed to Jane, Ivy, and Nick. "I saw many cats give birth when I was growing up in Trinidad, and I can tell you, Winky is a natural."

"That's nice," Jane said, "but her birthing days are over. As soon as the kittens are weaned, I'm having her spayed."

"Oh, Mom," Nick whined. "I want Winky to have more kittens."

"Sorry. This is as large as her family gets. We have to find homes for these six, so start asking around."

"Will do, missus. I think my friend Noni would like one."

"What about you, Ivy? Know anyone who'd like a kitten?"

But Ivy, apparently having lost interest, was gone.

Early the next day, Jane and Ivy drove to the north end of town and, after passing through rutted fields of gray-brown stubble, entered the forest that covered Mt. Munsee and started upward.

Heavy snow had begun to fall. Jane switched on the windshield wipers, but they did little good. The road was steep and narrow, and the snowflakes that seemed to be falling straight at them made driving even more difficult.

Ivy seemed not to have noticed. "This is so exciting. Come on, Jane, step on it. We'll never get there at this rate."

Jane remained silent, concentrating on the road. Soon its angle became less acute, though the tree branches hung lower, nearly touching the car.

Then the woods cleared and they found themselves on a delicate suspension bridge. Glancing out the window and down, Jane saw a deep gorge filled with a dizzying swirl of snow.

"How beautiful," Ivy said.

"And scary. I hate that grinding noise the tires make on the bridge."

They made it safely to the other side and

continued upward. Finally a sign appeared at the side of the road — MT. MUNSEE LODGE — and they emerged onto a narrow parking lot that ran the length of the lodge, a long, two-story rustic structure of dark wood.

The parking lot was nearly full. Jane had no sooner pulled into a space than she saw Adam in her rearview mirror, coatless, hurrying toward them from the lodge's entrance.

Jane rolled down her window.

"Welcome, welcome," Adam said, hopping from one foot to the other and rubbing his hands together. "You're just in time. We're all in the lounge having a get-acquainted breakfast."

Insisting on carrying their bags, he led the way into the lodge's reception area, a small room with a Formica counter. At each end of the wall behind the counter was a doorway leading into what must have been the lounge, for through them came the sounds of talk and laughter.

"I'll show you your rooms," Adam said.

"I can wait," Jane said, feeling she should join the group as soon as possible. "Though I can't speak for Ivy."

"I'll wait too," Ivy said eagerly, and Adam, clearly pleased with this response, led them into the lounge, in which small groups of people chatted. Against the back wall stood a table bearing bagels, Danish, juice, coffee, and tea.

Jane was aware of someone standing beside her and turned to see Daniel. He had been the first person she'd asked to serve as an instructor. "You made it," he said. "Looks pretty bad out there."

"Not so bad," Ivy answered for Jane, looking around. At that moment Ginny appeared at Daniel's arm. Ivy looked confused to see her. "Don't I . . . ?"

"Know me?" Ginny laughed. "I waited on you at lunch last week. I'm also" — she put her arm lovingly around Daniel's waist — "this handsome man's girlfriend."

"Ah," Ivy said. "Will you be teaching too?"

"No," Ginny scoffed. "I'm just along for the ride."

"Like my Johnny," Ivy said.

Ginny looked surprised. "Your boyfriend? He's coming here?"

"Mm-hm," Ivy responded smugly. "Should be here anytime now."

"I'd better say hello to the others," Jane said. She spotted another of her instructors, Arliss Krauss, standing nearby, chatting with an older man. Jane approached them.

Arliss, a senior editor at Millennium House, a publisher with which Jane had done a good bit of business, seemed pleased to see Jane, though with the habitually dour, deadpan Arliss, that wasn't saying much. She actually smiled a little as she greeted Jane, who noticed that Arliss was dressed for the lodge in brown wool slacks and a pretty tan corduroy shirt with the tails out.

"Good to see you, Arliss. Thanks so much for agreeing to do this at such short notice."

"No problem," Arliss said in her monotone voice. She turned to the man with whom she'd been chatting. He looked about sixty. He was tall and slim, with neatly trimmed graying brown hair. Jane saw kindness in the brown eyes behind wire-rimmed glasses. "Jane Stuart," Arliss said, "I'd like you to meet Brad Franklin."

So this was Brad Franklin. When Jane recruited Arliss, Arliss had recommended Brad, one of her authors, as an instructor. Brad, she told Jane, had written several novels under his own name but now made a handsome living ghostwriting novels for celebrities.

Brad said, "A pleasure, Jane," and shook her hand warmly. "Thanks for having me."

"Thank *you* for coming," Jane said, and excused herself to say hello to the others.

She decided to grab a bagel and a cup of coffee first, and made her way to the refreshment table, where Rhoda was straightening up.

"Morning, Jane darling. Glad you made it. Did you have any problems with the snow?"

"Nah. Piece of cake," Jane replied, smearing her bagel with cream cheese.

"Uh-uh-uh," came a whiny voice behind her, and forcing a smile, Jane turned.

"Hello, Bertha."

"Good to see you too, Jane." Chubby Bertha Stumpf pursed her lips and lightly fluffed her hair, which instead of its usual wrong shade of blond was now an odd assortment of blond and brown streaks. "How do you like the do?"

"Love it," Jane said. "How've you been, Bertha?"

Bertha tilted her head to one side and rolled her eyes heavenward. "Okay, I suppose. You know I finally persuaded that girl to accept *Shady Lady*."

"Oh? When was this?"

"Late Friday. She'll be calling you."

Jane guessed Bertha had done more bullying than persuading to get Harriet Green to accept her manuscript.

"Be a doll and see if you can get her to put a rush on my acceptance check, would you?" Bertha said.

Jane gave her a tight smile. "I'll see what I can do."

"We're going to have to have a serious talk about her, Jane. I can't go on with Bantam if they make me work with this girl."

"Stop calling her a girl, Bertha. She's a woman. She's also a very fine editor. And I'm afraid I won't be able to discuss your work here. We're here for the retreat, remember?"

Bertha clamped her mouth shut, as if a fury were building. "Of course I remember, Jane, I'm here because you asked me to be here. And let me tell you, getting out here from New York City was no easy game. Anyway, what I meant was that we could maybe discuss my career in our down moments — you know, when we're not teaching. Surely we won't be teaching every minute."

My *career* . . . If Bertha had used those words once since Jane had begun representing her five years earlier, she'd used them a hundred times. "You're right," Jane said placatingly. "I'm sure we'll find time

46

to talk in our down moments. Oh," she said, pointing across the room. "There's Vick Halleran. Excuse me, I have to say hello to him."

"Okay," Bertha said, though her tone made it clear she felt it was not okay at all.

Tough, Jane thought, making her way toward Vick.

Though Jane had never represented V. Sam Halleran, they traveled in the same circles and she had known him for years. Kenneth had also known and liked Vick, as his friends called him. Soft-spoken and self-effacing, short and plump, he was considered a guru of fiction writing. He traveled around the country almost constantly, presenting seminars and workshops, and had also published several best-selling books for writers.

"Jane," he cried, smiling sweetly, and they embraced. "You're looking wonderful, as beautiful as always." He took in her flowing mane. "Love that red hair," he said with gusto.

"Thanks, but it's auburn," she replied with a laugh. "Where's Jennifer?"

"Not sure," he said, and he and Jane scanned the crowd.

To Jane's surprise, Vick's wife, Jennifer Castaneda, had also agreed to serve as an instructor. Jennifer was a writer of Latina romance novels. She was, in fact, the leading writer of these novels, with four back-to-back *New York Times* best-sellers to her credit.

"There she is," Vick said, spotting her by one of the doorways to the reception room. "Jen —"

Jennifer looked up and smiled at them both. Some said the olive-skinned beauty was worthy of Hollywood, perhaps to star in a film version of one of her own novels, and looking at her now, Jane had to agree. Jennifer's rich brown hair was pulled back from her flawless brow, accentuating her large dark eyes, slightly tiptilted nose, and over-full pink lips. A snug linen jumpsuit in a becoming shade of celery accentuated her ample curves.

"Jane," she said in her breathy little-girl voice, approaching them. She kissed Jane on the cheek and embraced her. She smelled of jasmine.

"You're looking as gorgeous as ever," Jane said.

"You too," Jennifer said with a modest laugh. She pointed toward the doorway where Vick had spotted her. "I was just talking to one of the students. Come on, I'll introduce you."

Jane followed Jennifer, who Jane realized hadn't involved her husband at all in the conversation. Glancing behind her, Jane saw him trailing along. Jennifer approached a good-looking black-haired man in his mid-twenties. Of medium height, he was exceptionally slight, with effete, almost feminine features.

"Jane Stuart," Jennifer said, "this is Paul Kavanagh."

Paul's face lit up at the mention of Jane's name. He took Jane's hand and brought it to his lips. "It is an honor."

"Oh, my," Jane said with an embarrassed giggle. "Thanks very much."

"No, I must thank you." He came closer — too close for Jane's comfort. "When Adam told our group you had agreed to run this retreat," he said softly, "I couldn't believe my good fortune. You know, I've submitted my work to you a number of times, only to have you reject it." He lowered his gaze in desolation.

Jane felt herself flush. "I'm terribly sorry . . ."

"No, no," he said, putting up his hand. "You were absolutely right in your assessment. This week, however, I think you'll be quite impressed with what I've got to offer."

Already Jane couldn't stand this little twerp. "I'm sure I will," she said, hating herself for being such a phony, "though I must warn you, as I'll warn all the others, I'm not currently taking on any new clients." A lie, but a necessary one if she was to avoid awkward situations like this one.

Paul gave her a conspiratorial wink. "You have to say that; I understand. But wait until you see my work."

Jane told him it was nice to have met him, and couldn't get away quickly enough.

Vick came close to speak to her. "You did the right thing, telling him you're not taking on new clients. Otherwise every one of these people would be after you at the end of the retreat."

"I think this one will be after me anyway."

"Don't worry," Vick said. "I'll make sure he understands."

She thanked him and, turning away, caught Jennifer rolling her eyes at what Vick had just said. Jane, pretending she hadn't seen this, looked briskly about her. "Now, who else should I meet?"

"You can meet me," came a husky, rather coarse female voice from behind her. Jane spun around.

A tall, willowy woman with long ash-blond hair parted in the middle and a large beak of a nose walked straight up to Jane and put out her hand. "I'm your next million-dollar client."

Before Jane could react, the woman burst into raucous laughter. "I'm kidding. I'll be some other agent's first million-dollar client. I just heard you say you're not taking on anybody new."

"Right," Jane said. "And you are . . . ?"

"Carla Santino." She put out her hand and held Jane's in a viselike grip. "Waitress by day, future best-selling novelist by night."

"Waitress . . . Don't you —"

"Look familiar? Probably. I work at the Shady Hills Diner on Route Forty-six. I've probably waited on the whole town at some point or another. But I don't intend to be there much longer."

"Well, good for you," Jane said, eager to get away from Carla. Carla herself provided the getaway, pointing to a petite, mousy-looking woman who stood a couple of yards away, her hands clasped demurely in front of her, watching them. "Ellyn, get over here."

The mousy woman walked in tiny steps toward them and stopped. She wore a plain black skirt and a pink stretch blouse. Her curly dark hair looked as if it hadn't had the benefit of a good haircut in years. She looked, it occurred to Jane, not unlike a brunette Harpo Marx.

"Here's my fellow best-seller," Carla said, slapping the woman on the back. "Ellyn Bass — Jane Stuart."

"Glad to meet you, Ellyn. You're also from Shady Hills?"

"Yes," Ellyn replied. Her voice was high and squeaky. "But I don't work like Carla. I'm only a housewife."

"Don't ever say that," Jane said with a smile. "You're setting back the women's movement by about thirty years. Say, 'I don't work outside the home.' Much more p.c."

Ellyn nodded solemnly, as if completely unaware that Jane was being funny, or trying to be.

"Right," Jane said. "Any children, Ellyn?" she asked brightly.

"Five-year-old twin girls."

"And a handful, let me tell you," Carla put in. "I've served them enough to know. I've also served that husband of hers," she added, rolling her eyes. "Nice-looking, but useless."

Ellyn made a little frown but said nothing.

"What kind of writing are you doing, Ellyn?" Jane asked, now eager to get off the subject of Ellyn's family.

"I write romance novels." A dreamy, faraway look came into Ellyn's eyes. "I *adore* romance novels."

"How wonderful. Do you know we have two romance stars with us as instructors this week? Bertha — I mean Rhonda —"

"I know." Ellyn rose up on her heels in excitement. "Rhonda Redmond and Jennifer Castaneda. I've read every book they've ever written."

At that moment another woman joined them. Jane was enveloped in a cloud of expensive perfume.

"Who's written?" the woman asked. She spoke with an aristocratic lockjaw drawl and was dressed to match in an expensive-looking tan silk pantsuit. Jane guessed her to be around fifty. Her hair was a subtle gold, swept back from her well-tanned face and turning up slightly at her shoulders. Jane was immediately reminded of the actress Dina Merrill.

Jane opened her mouth to answer her, but the woman smiled apologetically. "How frightfully rude of me. I apologize for interrupting." She put out her hand. "Tamara Henley. I assume you're Mrs. Stuart?"

"Yes. Please call me Jane. Ellyn was just saying she's read all of Jennifer Castaneda's and Rhonda Redmond's books."

Tamara's smile half vanished and she regarded Ellyn pityingly. "Romance. Yes, well, that's fine for some. I'm here to work on something a bit more . . . ambitious. I know you'll be able to help me, Jane."

Ellyn stared down at the floor, duly put in her place.

Jane said, "Don't sell romance short, Tamara. It brings a lot of women pleasure. Most of it is beautifully written, too. People who don't read it aren't aware of that. They have a certain prejudice."

"Mm," Tamara replied, clearly bored. "As I said, fine for some." Then she gave Ellyn and Carla an intense gaze, as if willing them to go away. When they didn't, she looked again at Jane and smiled. "So nice to have met you, Jane. I'm sure we'll have our chance to *really* talk." She swept off toward the refreshment table.

"Snotty bitch," Carla said, as if she were about to spit. "That one I've never waited on at the diner, I'm sure of that. She'd never set foot in it." She cast Tamara a resentful look. "She's not even a member of the Midnight Writers."

"Oh?" Jane said. "Then how did she know about the retreat?"

"She's friendly with Rhoda and Adam. He told her about it."

Carla was watching Tamara at the refreshment table with a resentful look that made Jane uneasy.

"On to meet the rest of the students," Jane said cheerfully, and spotted three men she hadn't met chatting together and laughing in a corner of the room near the refreshment table. Jane made her way over to them and said hello to a bald man with a pleasant round face.

"Hello," he said. He had a warm smile that crinkled the corners of his deep blue eyes.

"Jane Stuart," she said, putting out her hand.

"Oh, Mrs. Stuart," he said, and dried his palm on his trousers before taking her hand and shaking it energetically. "A pleasure to meet you. Red Pearson." Before Jane could speak, he touched his bare head and said, "When I had hair, it was red. Let me introduce you to my friends here." He gestured toward an unusually unattractive man with pasty features and thinning, wiry, ginger-colored hair. "This is Larry Graham, our resident electrician."

Jane shook his hand. "A pleasure."

"Mutual," Larry said. " 'Course, I'm not here as an electrician. I've got a book I'm working on."

"I would hope so," Jane said with manufactured fervor, and turned to the third man in the group, a tiny, shriveled creature who was eighty if he was a day. He was so thin and gaunt that it occurred to Jane that he would break if she touched him. But she put her hand out just the same and received a surprisingly firm handshake in return.

"William Ives," he said in a thin, wavering voice. "Pleasure to know you."

Jane noticed Adam gesturing to her from the edge of the room. "Excuse me," she said to the three men, and made her way through the crowd to him.

"Jane, I think we should get started. What I usually do —"

But he was interrupted by a man who had suddenly appeared, a hunched, sour-looking older man with a thatch of white hair. "Somebody spilled coffee all over the table," he said in a low, droning voice.

"Then clean it up," Adam told him impatiently. "What do you expect me to do about it?"

The man skulked away.

"Who was that?" Jane asked softly.

Rhoda appeared at Adam's side, wearing a look of distaste. "That's Tom Brockman, the caretaker," she told Jane. "He's hopeless — a carryover from the lodge's previous owner. I've told Adam to fire him, but he refuses."

"Let's not get into that now," Adam said to Rhoda. "I hardly think it's appropriate."

"No, but it's appropriate for Tom to stick his hand in the till when it pleases him."

"Rhoda," Adam whispered angrily. "Stop it. You have no proof that he's ever done that. Really, this is wrong."

"Such a prisser," Rhoda said with a dismissive wave of her hand, and walked away.

"Anyway," Adam went on, his face red, "after the icebreaker we usually meet in the conference room next door. We go over how the retreat works, that sort of thing."

"I'd be happy to tell them how the retreat works," Jane said, "if I knew."

"Oh, right, this is all new to you. Okay, then I'll do that, and if you hear anything you'd like to do differently, speak up." Jane nodded, and Adam stepped back to address the entire group. "Ladies and gentlemen, if we could all go into the conference room, right through that door, I'd like to go over how the retreat will work."

Everyone headed for the door. Passing Jane, tall blond Carla muttered, "Finally," then saw Jane and forced a phony smile, revealing long, horselike teeth.

This character wasn't going to be easy, Jane thought. But then, the others didn't look easy, either.

What on earth had she gotten herself into?

Chapter Five

In her room, Jane took a stack of sweaters from her suitcase and placed them in the top drawer of the dresser. She reached for another stack of clothes, changed her mind, and went to the window.

The snow was still falling heavily. Through it Jane could make out the thick woods not far from the lodge. Through a break in the trees, she thought she saw a pond. If she had a chance, and if the weather allowed, she'd try to explore those woods while she was up here.

It was very quiet. The students were in their rooms, writing. In the conference room, Adam had announced the retreat's structure. Each morning, between breakfast and lunch, the students would write in their rooms. After lunch, during the first half of the afternoon, students would meet with their respective instructors (Jane had been assigned Larry Graham, the electrician) for their "one-on-ones," as Adam had put it. The second half of the afternoon students would have free, for socializing or whatever activities they chose.

Then would come dinner, followed by an evening group session at which students would be encouraged to read from their works-in-progress.

She stepped from the window and, though she hadn't finished unpacking, sat down at the foot of the bed and looked around the small room.

Right in front of her stood the dresser, long and low, with a mirror above. Atop the dresser was a vase containing an immense arrangement of fresh flowers. At the foot of the vase was the card she'd found attached: *Jane — Thank you so much for bailing me out. Your friend, Adam.* At the far left end of the dresser sat a Mr. Coffee machine — a nice touch, Jane thought.

Missing from the dresser — or from anywhere else in the room, for that matter — was a television set. How refreshing. Now if only there weren't a telephone on the bed stand, she thought, it would be perfect; but she knew, of course, that that wouldn't be possible.

The only other furniture was a small armchair to the left of the bed and a tiny desk and chair in one corner of the room. Nearby was the door to the bathroom.

Jane smiled. Rhoda had clearly added her own touches. In the bathroom Jane had found a basket of assorted scented soaps in the shape of pinecones and acorns. Here in the room itself Rhoda had added a holiday note: two large wreaths. A green one of fragrant eucalyptus and pine needles hung on the door to the corridor. On the wall to the right of the window hung a red one made of poinsettia flowers interwoven with cranberries.

She inhaled deeply, savoring the wreaths' mingled aromas. Then she was aware once again of the exquisite quiet. It really was quite lovely up here. She was surprised she hadn't been here before now. Rhoda had certainly mentioned Adam buying the lodge. Perhaps in the summer she and Stanley would come up for a night or two.

There was a boisterous knock on her door and Ivy burst in, face aglow. "He's on his way."

"Who?"

"Johnny, who do you think? He just called from his car. He should be here in about an hour."

But by lunchtime, two hours later, Johnny still hadn't arrived. Ivy sat glumly beside Jane at the large conference table that doubled as a dining table. Otherwise the chatter was lively and high-spirited, punctuated by laughter.

"Here you go, babe," Ginny said affectionately, setting down a plate of spaghetti and meatballs in front of Jane. Ginny had decided to make herself useful by helping to serve the meals — a job usually done by Adam and Rhoda alone. After all, Ginny had reasoned, she was a waitress. Jane watched Ginny set down a plate in front of Carla, who glanced at Ginny out of the corner of her eye but said nothing. Professional rivalry, Jane decided with an inward laugh, and started on a meatball.

The room grew quiet. Jane looked up. Johnny stood in the doorway, a thin coating of snow on his head and broad shoulders. In that brief moment, Jane happened to glance again at Carla and saw her lock glances with Johnny. It was as if, Jane thought, they had found each other by some sort of sonar. Quickly Jane looked at Ivy to see if she had noticed this exchange, but Ivy's eyes were also fixed only on Johnny. She jumped up with a joyful smile and ran to him, rising a little on her toes to give him a kiss. Then she turned around and giggled. "Everybody," she said, "this is Johnny, my boyfriend."

"Glad to know ya," Red called out, and tore into a roll.

Bertha, two seats down from Jane,

leaned over Ivy's now empty chair and whispered ominously to Jane, "Sparks are flying . . . and I don't mean between Ivy and Johnny. She'd better watch out."

Jane felt a lurching in the pit of her stomach and decided not to respond to Bertha's comment. She simply smiled. As she did so, she noticed Red Pearson watching Ivy intently as she made her way back to her seat.

Jane looked back at the doorway. Johnny was gone.

"Where did he go?" she asked Ivy.

"Upstairs to shower and change."

"Doesn't he want lunch?"

Ivy shook her head.

At the other end of the table, Larry Graham appeared to be holding court, entertaining William Ives and Tamara Henley. "Not me," Graham said pompously. "I'm taking my book right from today's headlines — literally."

"What do you mean?" Tamara drawled, and now the whole table was listening.

"I'm using that hijacked-bus story. Except that in my book, the bomb in his briefcase is real."

This created a flurry of chatter.

"You might say that about my book, too," Red Pearson said loudly. Darting a glance at Jane, he touched his bald head self-consciously. "You remember that story a few weeks ago about that social club in East Harlem that burned down?"

"I remember that," Ellyn said softly. "The Boriken Social Club."

"That's right," Red said. "Some nut started a fire right outside the club's only exit."

"Why did he do that?" Tamara asked.

"To get back at his girlfriend for cheating on him. She was inside the club."

"But what about all the other people?" Carla asked.

"He didn't care about them, apparently. There were nearly a hundred of them. They all panicked. A stampede. Eighty-seven of 'em either got trampled to death or got asphyxiated by the smoke."

"How awful," said Ginny, who had sat down next to Daniel to have her lunch.

"Horrible," Rhoda agreed.

"Yeah," Red said with relish. "That's what my book's about."

"No happy ending there," Carla said on a mouthful of spaghetti.

"Well, I'm taking certain licenses with it," Red said. "You'll see."

"I can hardly wait," Carla said, looking bored, and grabbed a roll.

After lunch, Adam drew Jane into the lounge to speak to her. "How do you think it's going?"

"Too soon to tell, I think. We certainly have an interesting assortment of people."

"True," Adam said, looking troubled. Through the door into the reception room, they saw Tom Brockman go outside carrying a snow shovel.

"The snow is supposed to be real heavy," Adam said. "Could be an accumulation of three feet or more."

"Does it matter?" Jane asked. "We'll all be busy inside."

"True, but I need to get down into town for food and such."

"Of course. I didn't think of that."

"We're fine for a few days, anyway."

Larry Graham entered the lounge and hovered nearby, clearly waiting to speak to one of them.

"Do you need me, Larry?" Adam asked.

"I'm waiting for Mrs. Stuart. She's my instructor."

Jane noticed that he had a spiral notebook in his hand. "Oh, yes, of course. I'm sorry, Larry. Let's go up to my room and talk about your project."

Chapter Six

Later that afternoon, as Jane left her room to go downstairs for dinner, Ivy emerged from her and Johnny's room directly across the hall.

"Johnny's changing. He'll be along in a few minutes." Ivy looked put out about something, her brow creased in a deep frown.

"Is something wrong, Ivy?"

Ivy sneezed.

"Bless you."

"Thanks. It's that awful man, Brockman."

"The caretaker? What about him?"

"He's impossible. Tell me something. Do you have wreaths in your room?"

"Wreaths? Yes, they're very pretty, aren't they? A nice holiday touch."

"I suppose they're pretty, but I'm allergic to them. I started sneezing the minute I got into my room. So after lunch I called down to ask that they be removed."

"And what happened?"

"Adam said he would send up this

Brockman creature. About an hour later, he banged on the door. When I told him what I wanted, he said — I swear — that he was too busy to take them down and that I should do it myself. Can you believe that?"

They headed down the stairway to the left of Jane's door. "That is rather rude," Jane said, surprised. "But not the end of the world, right?" Reaching the bottom of the stairs, they crossed the lounge and entered the conference room, where it seemed most of the others had already gathered.

"I mean," Ivy went on, apparently unable to let go of this issue, "how much trouble is it to take down two wreaths?"

"True," Jane said reasonably. "Which means it wouldn't have been a lot of trouble for you."

"Jane, that is not the point, and you know it. I am *allergic*, first of all. Disturbing the wreaths would have set me off sneezing all over again. Second, guests shouldn't have to do things like that — at least, not in good hotels."

"We're in Mt. Munsee Lodge, Ivy, not The Plaza. Why didn't you ask Johnny to take the wreaths down?"

Ivy didn't answer.

They were passing Tamara Henley at this point. She looked up. "Did you say wreaths?" she drawled. "Have you got those awful things in your room, too?"

"Yes," Ivy burst out, clearly glad to have a sympathizer. "A red one on the closet door and a green one on the door to the bathroom. Stink to high heaven — I'm allergic to them. The green one has some of that smelly eucalyptus in it. What do I look like, a koala?"

"Well, to tell you the truth . . ." Jane said, and burst out laughing.

"Oh, Jane," Ivy said. "You used to say that to me in school. Remember? You were always teasing me like that." She pushed out her bottom lip. "I'm about to cry."

"Me too," Jane said with a sniff, remembering their carefree college days. They seemed a lifetime ago. The two women had been so full of hope then; it seemed they could have anything they put their minds to. Now, looking back, Jane reflected that she had achieved much of what she had wanted: a fulfilling career, a husband who loved her, a beautiful child. Ivy had none of that, none of her dreams. Tears came to Jane's eyes.

"You *are* crying," Ivy said.

Tamara threw down her napkin in disgust. "Oh, really. Please, ladies, not at dinner."

Jane laughed through her tears and nodded.

"My wreaths are both green," Tamara said. "Tackiest things I've ever seen. Like some hideous Christmas card or something."

Jane looked across the table and saw Adam, who had apparently overheard this exchange, frowning.

"I asked the caretaker to remove them," Ivy told Tamara, "and he wouldn't. He was already at my door, but he refused to take them down. Can you believe such insolence?"

"I suppose I can live with mine, bad as they are," Tamara said with a languid wave, but Ivy had turned away.

Johnny had entered the room. He looked extremely handsome in a charcoal sport jacket over black slacks and a black silk T-shirt. Ivy's face bloomed in an expectant smile as she watched him make his way around the table. When he reached Carla, he stopped and she looked up, the corners of her lips turned up in the tiniest of smirks. Ever so lightly, his hand brushed her shoulder. Then he moved on, heading for the side of the table where Ivy stood.

Ginny, bearing a platter of roast chicken, stopped and spoke softly to Jane: "Ivy had better watch out or she's going to lose him. If she hasn't already."

Taking her seat, Jane found herself deeply troubled by what she had seen and by Ginny's remark. Poor Ivy had been hurt or disappointed by men all her life, beginning with her father, who had walked out on her mother when Ivy was thirteen. Ira, Ivy's ex-husband, had had affair after affair during their marriage and then abandoned her as well, leaving Ivy to raise their daughter, Marlene, alone. Jane didn't want Ivy to be hurt again.

But Jane saw no way to prevent it if it was going to happen, especially when she saw Ivy watching Johnny make his way toward her, a hurt expression on her face.

Later, as dinner was ending, Tom Brockman appeared in the doorway from the lounge. He wore a bulky down parka that appeared soaked through. The room grew quiet.

"Snow's stopped," he droned. "But the bridge collapsed under the weight." There was a quick collective intake of breath. "Was tryin' to drive down into town for supplies. Nearly drove into the gorge."

Everyone broke into animated chatter.

"What are we going to do?" Arliss said in her droning voice that was not unlike Brockman's.

"Yes," Paul Kavanagh chimed in, "this is terrifying."

Adam rose from his chair. "People, people — please. There's nothing to worry about. There's another road. It's old and hasn't been used in a while, but it's there, and it goes down the other side of the mountain. I'll arrange for it to be plowed, but it will take a while. In the meantime, we've got plenty of food and supplies. So let's just enjoy our retreat, shall we?" He shot Tom Brockman a withering look.

"This is unacceptable," Ivy said to Jane a few minutes later in the lounge, where they sat side by side on a sofa.

Jane laughed. "Why, have you got someplace to go?"

"No, you know I haven't. It's just that we're . . . *stranded* here. What if there's an emergency and one of us needs to get down the mountain?" Ivy's eyes widened. "What if *you* need to get home because something has happened to Nick, heaven forbid."

"Calm down, all will be fine. Have a seat. The group reading is starting soon."

Ivy sat, twisting her fingers in her lap.

"Ivy," Jane said in a low voice, unsure how to begin. "Is Johnny . . . I mean, do you think he's really right for you?"

Ivy turned and looked at Jane as if she'd gone mad. "What are you talking about?"

"I don't know. It's just that he seems, well, interested in other women. Do you think he's really committed to you?"

"Oh, Jane," Ivy said solemnly, "absolutely. Johnny loves me as much as I love him. I know I haven't always had very good judgment in men, but of this I am sure. Johnny adores me. I do intend to have a heart-to-heart with him, though. I mean, he is a man," she said with a little laugh, rolling her eyes skyward. "I don't expect him to ignore a beautiful woman when he sees one, but he's got to be more discreet about it. Keep it to himself, you know?"

Jane nodded uneasily, her lower lip between her teeth. Looking around the lounge, she noted that Johnny was absent.

She directed her attention to Ellyn Bass, who stood at the front of the room, having bravely volunteered to be the first to read from her work-in-progress.

It was a historical romance set in eighteenth-century Scotland. In this scene, the hero was about to make love to a woman other than the book's heroine.

"Oh, no," Bertha suddenly blurted out, standing. "Cut. Unh-unh. No can do."

Ellyn gaped at her.

"You see," Bertha said, addressing the entire group, "in a historical romance, once the hero and heroine meet, they will fight, come together, be thrust apart — the natural rhythm of love — but the hero must *never, never* sleep with another woman."

"That's a crock," Jennifer Castaneda, sitting at the other end of the room, said matter-of-factly, and everyone grew very still. "Maybe in your books, Berth—"

"Rhonda," Bertha corrected her quickly. She never used her real name in public.

"Rhonda," Jennifer said, rolling her eyes. "But that's all so . . . eighties."

"Eighties!" Bertha's face grew red beneath its streaked blond crown. "I'll have you know that I am a bigger name now than I was in the eighties. To what do you attribute that?"

"People are ridiculously loyal to the oldies. I don't follow any of those silly rules in my books, and I think you'll find they're outselling yours."

Jane looked on, horrified, as if she were watching a car wreck.

"I think *you'll* find you're wrong," Bertha

said viciously. "Besides, your books aren't even historicals, they're contemporaries — Hispanic contemporaries."

"*Latina. La-ti-na* contemporaries. That's the whole point. I'm writing what readers want today — a good story, without those foolish category rules."

"Category!"

Adam jumped up. "Now, now, ladies," he said with a laugh, his face an even deeper red than Bertha's, "I think everyone here agrees that you are both giant names in your field."

"Oh, she's a giant all right," Jennifer said.

Brad Franklin let out a guffaw, and Bertha turned livid eyes on him. His face grew instantly serious.

Adam cleared his throat loudly and addressed Ellyn with a wan smile. "You should be very proud that your book has been able to arouse such controversy already."

"That's right, Ellyn," Jennifer said, "you write 'em how you want. Your readers will love you for it. Before you know it, you'll be the next . . . Bertha Stumpf!"

William Ives, looking shrunken in the corner, said, "Who's Bertha Stumpf?"

Bertha surveyed the group in horror.

"Well, I — I'm certainly not —" And she stomped out of the room.

"Good," Jennifer cried triumphantly. "Now we can continue without any more interruptions."

Ellyn chose not to read any further. Paul Kavanagh read next from his novel, an artsy coming-of-age story about a boy who, fearing he might be gay, went to see his priest.

"Ha," Ivy burst out.

"Ivy," Jane whispered fiercely.

"I'm sorry," Ivy called to Paul. "It just strikes me as funny."

Paul glared at her, openmouthed. "What's funny about it?"

"It's so obvious the boy is you."

Without a word, Paul turned and left the room.

Rhoda jumped up from her chair. "People, people, listen to me. We can't do this. We have to be considerate of one another's feelings or this isn't going to work. Constructive criticism only, please. Delivered . . . sensitively."

"Excu-u-use *me*," Ivy said.

Tom Brockman appeared at the side of the room and motioned to Adam, who got up and followed Tom into the reception room. As Carla Santino read from her mainstream women's novel, the sounds of Tom and Adam arguing heatedly could be clearly heard.

Forty-five minutes later, Jane, utterly exhausted, rose at the end of the group reading. Daniel and Ginny approached her.

"That was . . . interesting," Daniel said with a wicked grin. "Do you think Bertha will be all right?"

"Of course," Jane blustered. "She throws hissy fits like that all the time and forgets about them the next day. You two want to come up to my room for some coffee?"

"Sure," Ginny and Daniel said, and so did Ivy, suddenly standing at Jane's elbow. Jane would rather have taken a break from Ivy, but she saw no way to exclude her, so the four of them went to Jane's room, where she made coffee in the Mr. Coffee machine on the dresser.

Ivy took the chair behind the desk in the corner of the room, Jane dropped into the armchair, and Ginny and Daniel sat on the bed.

"This is all turning out pretty awful, isn't it?" Ivy said, and they all turned to look at her. "I mean, first the bridge collapsing, then that horrible reading just now. And then that repulsive Red Pearson made not one but two passes at me. What would ever make him think I'd be interested in *him?* Bald as a cue ball," she muttered.

Jane thought of suggesting that perhaps Red had noticed Johnny's interest in Carla and therefore deduced that Ivy was available, but of course Jane restrained herself.

"You know who's awfully sweet, though?" Ivy went on. "That little William Ives. Isn't he the cutest thing?"

Ginny looked aghast. "You mean that shriveled-up man with the skinny head?" She shuddered.

"Oh, come on, Ginny. Make believe he's your grandfather."

"My grandfather happens to be an exceptionally handsome man."

"You're being very . . . superficial — yes, that's the word. I think he's sweet, that's all. I also," Ivy went on, leaning forward a little, "had a very interesting chat with that Brad Franklin, the ghostwriter. *Very* interesting."

"How so?" Jane asked. "What did he say?"

"Never you mind," Ivy replied smugly.

Jane was about to object to Ivy's sudden discretion when there was a violent knock on the door. Jane hurried to open it and found Rhoda standing in the corridor. She bustled in, obviously disturbed about something.

"You're not going to believe this," she said. "You know Tom's room is downstairs next to the storage room?"

They all looked at her blankly.

"Well, it is. Anyway, Tom just told Adam that there are people *carrying on* in the storage room."

"Really?" Ivy asked avidly. "Who?"

"I don't know," Rhoda said, exasperated, and turned to Jane. "What should I do?"

Jane's eyes grew wide and she hunched her shoulders in a shrug. "Beats me. Let Adam handle it. It's his lodge. He can look into it if he likes." And she thought, *I've got a pretty good idea who's in there.*

For a moment Rhoda stood there, staring. Then she nodded resolutely, turned, and hurried out of the room and down the stairs.

"I'm not much in the mood for coffee after all," Ginny said, and Daniel nodded in agreement.

"I guess I'm about ready to turn in," Jane said, and was grateful when Ivy got the hint and left with them.

Jane took a long hot shower, put on her nightgown, brushed her teeth, combed her hair, and settled on the bed with a manuscript she'd brought from the office. Just as she turned over the title page, there was a knock on the door.

"Who is it?"

"Jane, it's me, Ivy."

Jane let out a great sigh. "Coming." Throwing on her robe, she went to the door and opened it. At the far end of the corridor, Tamara Henley emerged from her room, crossed to the room Carla and Ellyn were sharing, and knocked on their door.

Ivy walked into Jane's room and shut the door. "You know, that Tamara is totally cold and unfeeling. It's really bothering me. That nice William Ives can vouch for it."

"Vouch for what? What did she do?"

"Right after I left here before, I went downstairs to see if there was anything to eat in the kitchen. Tamara and William were in the conference room and we had some fruit together. Anyway, we got to chatting about this and that, and somehow I got on to how I lost Marlene. Well. Tamara made it abundantly clear that she didn't want to hear anything about it. Don't you think that's cold?"

"Yes, I do. I don't blame you for being hurt. Ivy, where's Johnny?"

"I think he's in the lounge, watching the news. Can you believe there are no TVs in these rooms? Speaking of the news," Ivy swept on, sitting on the bed, "have you heard anything more about that bus hi-jacking story?"

"No, why?"

Ivy shook her head, frowning, then yawned mightily. "I'm going to bed. Good night, Jane."

Bewildered, Jane let Ivy out and watched her enter her room across the hall. Then she resumed her position on the bed, took up her manuscript, and started to read.

Ten minutes later there was another knock.

"Oh, for goodness' sake." She went to the door. "Ivy, I thought you were going to bed."

"It's me, Daniel."

"Daniel?" She opened the door and he walked in.

"Sorry to bother you, Jane, but there's something I think you'd better know. A few minutes ago I was walking through the lounge. Ivy was there, sitting and talking with Larry Graham. Suddenly the door to the storage room opened and out came Johnny and Carla. You should have seen Ivy's face. Poor thing."

"Did Johnny see her?"

"Yes, he gave her a quick glance and walked past her as if she didn't matter in the least."

Poor Ivy. What would happen now?

"And as if that wasn't enough," Daniel went on, "as I was coming upstairs, I passed Tom Brockman. He had a real stormy look and I wondered what was bothering him. Then I bumped into Adam, who said he'd just reprimanded Tom for being rude to the guests."

She remembered Ivy's wreath incident.

"Adam told Tom that if he didn't lose his attitude fast, he'd have to leave as soon as the old road was plowed." Daniel looked troubled. "But it was the Carla and Johnny thing I felt you should know about."

"Thanks. I appreciate it. Not that I can do anything about it, but thanks."

She saw him out, took one look at the bed, and knew she was too tired to read now. She put the manuscript on the dresser, climbed under the covers, and switched off the lamp. A short time later, as she was drifting off to sleep, she was aware of the sound of people yelling. Slowly she came awake and realized they were Ivy and Johnny. She couldn't make out what they were saying, just that Ivy was crying, pleading.

This went on for some time. Finally it became quiet, and Jane drifted into an uneasy sleep.

Chapter Seven

The atmosphere at breakfast was subdued, as if everyone had a hangover. Adam announced that the plowing of the old road had begun but would take a while.

As Jane sat down, Arliss took the seat beside her.

"Jane, what on earth was all that noise last night?"

"I don't know, Arliss."

"It was coming from that floozy's room —"

"Don't call my friend a floozy."

"It was coming from Ivy and Johnny's room, which is right next to mine and across the hall from yours. How could you not have heard it?"

"I didn't say I didn't hear it. I just said I didn't know what it was."

Arliss regarded her for a moment. "I see. Being discreet, are we? Well, it's unacceptable, Jane. I'm here as a favor to you, but this is my vacation and I expect certain standards to be met."

"All right, Arliss. If it will make you feel better, I'll ask Ivy to be more considerate.

Couldn't you have done that?"

"Of course I could have. But it's not my job. You're the director of this thing, and it's your responsibility to make sure it goes smoothly. So far, I'm sorry to say, you've done a lousy job."

Before Jane could respond, Arliss got up and walked away, taking a seat at the far end of the table. Almost immediately, Daniel took her place. "Morning," he said brightly. "What was all that commotion last night?"

"None of your business," blurted Ivy, who sat directly across from them, glaring.

Daniel, shocked, took a quick bite of his croissant. Ivy got up and began to walk around the table. She stopped at the coffee urn, poured a cup, and headed back to her seat. As she passed behind Carla, she stopped, stepped closer to the table, and dropped the coffee right in front of Carla, who gasped and jumped up. "You bitch," she screamed. "You deliberately spilled that on me. I'm burned." She slapped Ivy hard across the face, then ran from the room.

Everyone was silent.

"Oops," Ivy said.

"Oh, Ivy," Jane said, throwing down her napkin, and hurried from the room to make sure Carla was all right. Upstairs, she knocked on Carla's door and Carla opened it. She had already removed her jeans, and she pointed to angry red marks on her thighs.

"Look at this. That bitch burned me. Can you believe it?"

Jane didn't know what to say.

"I know she hates me because she saw Johnny and me come out of the storage room last night, but that's too bad for her."

"You can't blame her for being upset," Jane said, then quickly added, "Not that I condone what she just did."

"It's not going to make any difference," Carla said, pulling on a fresh pair of jeans. "Stupid fool thinks Johnny cares about her. He was laughing at her when he was with me."

Jane felt a pang of hurt for her friend. Sadly she turned and left Carla's room.

Later, during writing time, Jane was in the lounge reading the manuscript she'd tried to read the night before, when Ellyn Bass timidly approached her. "Jane, could I talk to you for a minute?"

"Sure, Ellyn. What's up?"

"Something's bothering me. Last night Tamara came to my room and told me I have writing talent but that I shouldn't waste it on romance. Jane, I *love* romance. I love reading it and I love writing it. It really hurt my feelings when she said that to me."

"I don't blame you for feeling hurt," Jane said. "She shouldn't have said that to you — though I suppose she meant well, in her way."

"Aren't we all supposed to be encouraging? Supportive of each other's efforts, like Rhoda said?"

"Yes, definitely. I'm glad you mentioned this to me. I'll speak to Tamara."

Ellyn smiled. "Thanks, Jane. I'm really enjoying this retreat."

"Good, Ellyn, I'm glad." Jane smiled as she watched Ellyn leave the room.

Suddenly Ivy had taken Ellyn's place, and Jane felt her smile melt. Ivy looked miserable, her hair tousled, her clothes rumpled. She wore no makeup.

"Oh, Jane," she said on a little cry, sitting down beside her friend. "It's so awful."

"What is?" Jane asked, remembering the yelling coming from her and Johnny's room.

"I saw Johnny come out of that storage closet with Carla. I told him so last night, but he didn't care. He actually got mad at *me.*" Carefully she raised her sweater to reveal an angry black-and-blue mark.

Jane sat up in alarm. "How did you get that?"

"He hit me," Ivy said, and started to cry. "He hits me a lot, Jane." She hung her head, staring into her lap. "He always hits me in places where it won't show."

Jane sat up, incensed. "Then you should have gotten rid of him a long time ago. How dare he hit you? You're well rid of him."

Ivy gave her head a little shake. "No, I'm not, Jane. He's all I have." She met Jane's gaze, her eyes brimming with tears. "Do you think it's that easy for me to find men?"

"But isn't no man better than one who hurts you?" Jane asked gently.

"No." Ivy paused, collecting her thoughts. "He got so furious at me for challenging him that he threatened to leave here with Carla the minute the road was clear."

"I don't know what to tell you, Ivy. If it were me, I'd let him go."

"But you're not me, Jane, don't you get it? You've never been me. You're beautiful and successful and funny and smart, and you got Kenneth, the man you wanted.

The man who loved you and treated you like a queen. And if he hadn't been killed you'd still have him. Me, I got Ira, who constantly cheated and finally left me because I was 'stupid and boring.' You never met the men I dated after Ira. Each one was worse than the one before. Then I met Johnny. He's part of my new life in New York. I love him. He doesn't mean to hurt me, he just has a wicked temper. And he always says he's sorry afterward. I know he means it. I — I can't lose him, Jane. What am I going to do?" she asked miserably, and buried her face in her hands.

Jane simply shook her head. "I'm sorry, Ivy. I won't advise you about how to keep a monster like that."

Ivy looked again at Jane, this time as if she'd never seen her before. "You're not my friend, not really. You don't want me to be happy. I see that now. If I lose Johnny, you'll be glad, because you'd rather I had nobody than someone like him. You're a snob, Jane." She jumped up and ran from the room.

Jane sat very still. That last accusation had hit hard, and hurt. It took all of her energy to rise and make her way through the empty conference room and into the kitchen for a much-needed cup of coffee.

As she filled a cup, she heard people entering the conference room and realized they were Vick Halleran and Jennifer Castaneda. They seemed to be arguing about something.

"Vick, I came in here to get some writing done," came Jennifer's breathy girl-woman voice. "Do you think you could leave me alone for a little while?"

"You never want to spend any time with me," Vick whined. "You just wanted to get away from me. Maybe you wish you'd come to the retreat with *Henry*."

Jane stood stock-still. If she emerged from the kitchen now, they would know she'd heard them, which would be too embarrassing to bear. So she stayed where she was, listening.

"Oh, shut up," Jennifer said. "I've told you a million times that's over."

Jane recalled that Jennifer's agent was Henry Silver, for whose agency, coincidentally, Jane and Kenneth had once worked.

There was the sudden sound of a chair scraping the floor. "I don't believe it's over, Jennifer. But whether it is or isn't," Vick said icily, "if you try to divorce me, I'll take you for all you're worth."

"Really?" Jennifer sounded amused. "And how would you justify that?"

"You'd be nothing if it weren't for me, if it weren't for all I've taught you about writing. You used me . . . and now I'll use you."

Then there was silence. Jane waited a good two minutes, then intentionally made some noise to signal her presence. Cup in hand, she bustled out, pretending to be surprised to find Jennifer typing away on her notebook computer.

"Hello," Jane said. Jennifer gave her a tight smile and returned her attention to her computer screen.

Feeling a headache coming on, Jane retrieved her manuscript from the lounge and took it up to her room. She had just finished reading chapter one when a loud *pop*, a sound she recognized immediately as a gunshot, exploded in the hall, just outside her door.

Chapter Eight

Heart thumping, Jane hurried to her door, opened it a crack, and peeked out. A middle-aged man in a tan overcoat, sloppily obese and sweating profusely, ran past her room, holding a gun out in front of him. Jane peered down the length of the corridor in time to see Johnny run down the stairs. The man scrambled after him.

Across the corridor, Ivy's door opened and she stood there, looking badly shaken, her blue eyes huge.

"Ivy, what's going on?" Jane demanded.

Without responding, Ivy shut her door.

Other doors along the corridor were thrown open and alarmed faces peered out.

Adam came running up the stairway to the left of Jane's room. "Everyone stay in your rooms," he shouted down the corridor. He saw Jane and came into her room. "We've got to call the police."

"Yes. I'll call Stanley." She rang him at the station and found him in his office. She told him what had just happened, that a man with a gun had run through the lodge, chasing Johnny.

"Jane, I can't get up there until the road is plowed. I told you Johnny was no good. I'm sure there's nothing more to worry about. The two of them are probably far into the woods by now."

"But how could that man have gotten up here?"

"He must have hiked up one of the trails — there are lots of them. He was a heavyset man, you said?"

"Yes, that's right."

Stanley let out a little laugh. "He must have wanted Johnny pretty bad."

"I don't think this is funny," Jane said in alarm.

"No, of course not. Sorry, Jane. I'll see what I can do to hurry up the plowing and get up there."

Jane hung up the phone, an image of Johnny running through the snowy woods in her mind.

Adam said, "Jane, I want to talk to Ivy, see what she knows about this."

"Don't you think we should wait for Stanley?"

Adam ignored this, leaving Jane's room and crossing to Ivy's. He banged on her door.

"Go away," she shouted from inside.

"Ivy, open the door. We need to talk to you. Please."

After a few moments they heard her shuffling steps, and then the door opened. They walked past her, Jane closing the door.

"Ivy," Jane said, "who was that man chasing Johnny?"

"I don't know." Ivy sat down on the bed, the very picture of dejection.

"I think you do, Ivy."

"I don't know who he is, Jane. I only know that Johnny's been trying to get away from him. I don't know why." She looked up miserably into Jane's eyes. "Johnny was never really going away this weekend. I used you, Jane. I knew Johnny was looking for a place to hide from that man. When you told me about the retreat, I realized it would be perfect. So I got you to invite me, and then I convinced you to let Johnny come. I'm sorry."

"It doesn't matter, Ivy," Jane said sadly. "He's gone now."

The phone in Jane's room began to ring. Jane hurried across the hall and grabbed it.

"Hello, hello, missus," came Florence's lilting Trinidadian voice. "How are you holding up, all stranded?"

"Florence," Jane said, "you have no idea."

"I see . . ." Florence said, though she of course didn't. "I wanted to report in, tell you that Nicholas is fine, and so are Winky and the kittens. We're working on names, but no final decisions have been made. Is the old road clear yet? It seems everyone in town is talking about you all stuck up there."

"They're still working on the road." Jane thought of something. "Florence, has anyone come to the house looking for me or Ivy?"

"Why, yes, missus, as a matter of fact someone did. Yesterday. A man."

"What did he look like?"

"Kind of overweight, missus, in a light-colored coat, like a trench coat. Maybe in his forties. He asked for Ivy Benson. Why?"

"What did you tell him?"

"That she was at the retreat, of course. Why, missus? Did I do something wrong?"

"No, it's all right, Florence. I'd better go now. Give Nick a kiss for me, okay?"

"Will do."

As Jane hung up, Rhoda appeared in the doorway. She turned when Adam emerged from Ivy's room.

"Come on," Jane said to them both. "I want to see something."

"Where?" Adam asked.

"Outside."

Jane led the way along the corridor to the stairs down which Johnny and the gunman had run. They went out through the door at the end of the building and emerged onto the snow-covered lawn. Jane immediately spotted two sets of footprints. "This way."

The prints led into the woods, but there was no trail here, and they were quickly lost in the tangle of brush. Returning to the lodge, Jane wondered if the man with the gun had caught up with Johnny.

Not surprisingly, no one got any writing done that morning, and lunch was abuzz with speculation. Somehow Adam had found out it was Ellyn Bass's birthday, and after lunch he and Ginny brought out an Entenmann's coffee cake studded with candles, along with some fruit punch. Adam sent Tom into the kitchen for ice, but Tom reappeared a few moments later.

"Mr. Forrest, the icemaker is malfunctioning again. The ice cubes have melted together into a blob. Do you have the ice pick?"

"No," Adam replied impatiently, "what would I be doing with the ice pick?" He went into the kitchen himself, and they could hear him rummaging in drawers, then, "Damn."

He reappeared, looking frustrated. "I have no idea where it is. Tom, get a screwdriver from the supply closet."

Tom did, and soon Adam was hacking away at the cubes.

The cake and punch went a long way toward lifting the group's spirits. When it was time for the one-on-one sessions, everyone bustled off quite happily, almost as if nothing unusual had happened that morning at the lodge.

After lunch, Jane met with Larry Graham in her room for their one-on-one session.

"I didn't write anything this morning," he announced, falling into the armchair near the bed.

Jane sat behind the desk. There was something different about him, Jane noticed, then realized it was his hair, that unruly mass of thinning orange fuzz. He appeared to have tried to part it in the middle — for what reason, she couldn't imagine — and had achieved a thoroughly unpleasant effect. He sat watching her.

"I suppose I can't blame you for not getting any writing done today," she said pleasantly, "what with all that's gone on."

"Yeah, that's it," he said, a smile breaking over his coarse features.

It was suddenly somehow clear to Jane that that hadn't actually been the reason, but that he was happy to use it as his excuse.

"What was that all about?" he asked. "With Johnny and that guy with the gun. Do you think Johnny is some kind of Mafia figure? Who was the other guy?"

Jane shook her head and tried to smile. "I'm sure I have no idea." She wanted him to stop talking about this.

"I intend to find out. I'm going to follow their footprints into the woods, figure out where they went."

"Already tried that," she said, and she could tell by his quick series of blinks that this had surprised him. "There's no trail where they ran into the woods, just sticks and underbrush. The prints get lost. Besides," she added, shivering, "I don't think we necessarily want to know what happened. That's one trail I've decided I don't want to follow."

"Mm," he said thoughtfully. "Trails . . . You know, there are some trails you can't see . . ."

What on earth was he talking about? "All righty, then," she said briskly, getting to her feet, "if you'll forgive me, I'll use the rest of our time for some reading — since you haven't written anything new for us to go over. You don't object, do you?"

"No, no, not at all," he said, still oddly preoccupied, and she showed him out, relieved to be rid of him.

She went to the window and gazed out into the woods, dark and forbidding on this bleak gray day. She glanced about her room and it seemed oppressive suddenly, shabby and depressing. She had to get out of there. Taking up her manuscript, she left the room and went down to the lounge, which was blessedly empty. She settled into a big leather chair near the built-in bookcases at the back of the room, sighed deeply, and resumed her reading.

She heard footsteps and, with a sense of dread, looked up into Bertha's pudgy face.

"Hello, Jane," Bertha said rather coolly.

Was she going to apologize for that scene with Jennifer? Hardly likely, knowing Bertha.

"Jane," she said, falling onto the sofa facing Jane's chair, "I think this is a good time to talk about my career."

Jane felt a kind of sinking nausea in the

pit of her stomach. "Actually, this isn't a good time. I've got some work to do, and before you know it, it will be time for dinner."

Bertha looked at the watch on her chubby wrist. "It's hours till dinner. You just don't want to talk to me."

Bingo. "No, that's not it at all, Bertha. It's that I'm very busy, running the retreat and all. As I think I told you, there really isn't time to discuss your career during the retreat."

"That's not what you said at all," Bertha whined. "You agreed we'd find time to talk in our 'down moments.' "

Giving up, Jane set down the manuscript on the coffee table. "All right, let's talk about your career."

"Hello, ladies."

Jennifer Castaneda swept into the room. She wore a snowy white fisherman's knit sweater over black leggings. Jane reflected again on what a beauty this woman was, sleek and sinuous. She sat down beside Bertha and good-naturedly patted her knee. "I'm sorry about those things I said about your books."

Bertha looked amazed. "Why . . . thank you."

Would Bertha apologize back? Jane wondered. She doubted it.

She was right. Bertha just sat there, an expectant look on her face. Jane knew she was wishing Jennifer would leave.

But Jennifer crossed her legs and settled more comfortably on the sofa. "You've got to admit, though, that historical romances and contemporary romances are totally different."

Bertha drew in her breath to respond. Jane wasn't going to give her that chance. "I've been admiring that beautiful sweater, Jennifer. You know, I'm a knitter." When Jennifer looked surprised, Jane went on, "Mm-hm, I even belong to a knitting club. We call ourselves the Defarge Club. Cute, huh?"

Both Jennifer and Bertha had completely blank expressions.

"Madame Defarge was a character in *A Tale of Two Cities*."

Still the vacant looks.

"Surely you've both heard of Charles Dickens."

"Yes, of course," Bertha said, and shifted impatiently.

"Anyway," Jane hurried on, "I've made sweaters not unlike that. They're a lot of fun to do, all those cables and bobbles and things."

Jennifer gave Jane a wondering look. At that moment Tamara Henley entered the lounge from the stairs, passing through on her way to the conference room. "Hello," she drawled.

The three women smiled and returned the greeting, watching her pass through the room. The minute she was gone, Jennifer giggled and leaned closer to the two other women. "Speaking of clothes," she whispered cattily, "did you get a load of what Mrs. Gotrocks has got on? The woman does *not* know how to dress."

"Really?" Bertha said. "What was she wearing? I didn't notice."

"How could you not notice?" Jennifer said. "That gray skirt and lavender top. Clash city." She gave a little shrug. "I guess it just goes to show that money doesn't guarantee good taste."

Jane didn't like where this conversation was going. Sitting with these two was making her feel increasingly anxious. "Oh," she said suddenly, "I just remembered I've got to call my nanny about something. You'll both excuse me?"

Bertha, looking positively betrayed, stared at Jane as she rose from her chair.

Jennifer said, "Sure."

Jane hurried out of the lounge and up

the stairs. She met Adam coming down.

"Hello, Jane. I've decided to throw another little party tonight. After that business with Johnny and the man with the gun, I figure everyone could use some special treatment."

"I think that's an excellent idea."

"Good. Rhoda and I will be hosting it in the conference room after the group reading."

She told him she'd see him later and made it to her room, where she actually managed to finish reading the manuscript.

Chapter Nine

At dinner, Jane, sitting between William Ives and Daniel, glanced around the room, wondering where Ivy was. As if reading her thoughts, Daniel whispered, "Isn't Ivy coming to dinner?"

"I don't know," Jane replied, and at that moment Ivy appeared in the doorway.

She looked like hell, as if she hadn't bathed or changed her clothes since yesterday. She made her way over to Jane, William, and Daniel and took the empty seat next to William. Watching Ivy sit down a little too carefully, Jane wondered if she'd been drinking.

The atmosphere was subdued — Adam, Rhoda, and Ginny serving, everyone quietly eating. Adam, crossing the room with a tray, gave Jane an imploring look. She nodded.

"Well," she burst out sunnily. "How are everyone's stories coming along?"

They all looked at her, wary expressions on their faces.

Finally William looked up and smiled at Jane. "I think mine's a real humdinger," he said in his thready voice. "Maybe I'll get myself one of those movie deals. But I've got to executive produce."

Everyone laughed, the atmosphere loosening up.

"*I've* got a hell of a story," Ivy suddenly announced. The room grew silent again. Everyone watched her, waiting.

"Mm-hm," she continued matter-of-factly, spearing a piece of chicken and putting it in her mouth. "It's going to put someone in jail for years and years."

Again the uneasy silence. Jane didn't blame Ivy for feeling bitter toward Johnny and was happy that her friend was rid of him, but she didn't like the way this conversation was going.

"What about you, Carla?" Jane asked.

Carla looked up and scowled at Jane, who refused to be intimidated.

"How is your novel coming along?"

"Fine," Carla said brusquely, and looked away. "Pass the butter, please."

Jane gave up. The remainder of the meal was eaten in virtual silence.

The atmosphere of that evening's group session made Jane nervous, as if the air itself were charged.

Tamara read from her novel, about a

woman dying of breast cancer. Red Pearson ripped it to shreds, calling it maudlin and melodramatic.

When he read from his own novel based on the Boriken Social Club tragedy, Tamara got him back by loudly scoffing at least three times.

William Ives, in his thin, shaky voice, read a passage from his novel about a lost woodsman. To Jane's surprise, it was extremely well written. She noticed Arliss, William's instructor, nodding approvingly at the other end of the room. Jane wondered, perhaps uncharitably, if Arliss had rewritten William's material. Brad Franklin, as if reading Jane's thoughts, called out, "Sounds like your teacher helped you with your homework."

"What is that supposed to mean?" William demanded.

Brad laughed, his shoulders rising and falling once. "It's obvious. Arliss rewrote your stuff. Or maybe she just wrote it, saved you the trouble of doing anything at all."

A hush descended upon the room. Arliss was watching Brad with a shocked, hateful look in her eyes. "That remark was totally uncalled for, Brad," she said, "and I resent it immensely."

Brad laughed again. "Sorry, sorry. I was only joking."

"You know," Ivy said, and everyone turned to her, "I think Brad is the last person who should object to someone's writing being 'ghosted,' since that's exactly what he does for a living."

Brad's face grew serious. "I just told you," he said tightly, "I was joking."

Ivy appeared to ignore this. "Damn cushy setup," she muttered. "Cushier than people think."

Brad gave her a surprised, murderous look.

Paul Kavanagh read more of his coming-of-age novel, a passage in which the protagonist experienced his first homosexual encounter. In the middle of the reading, Red yelled out that he hadn't come to this retreat to hear porno. This time Paul, who seemed to have girded himself for blows such as this, simply finished reading and took his seat.

Ellyn Bass read lovingly from her romance, dwelling on the heavy Scottish accents. Tamara rolled her eyes. To Jane's surprise, Jennifer criticized the passage, saying that dialect would make her book difficult to read. Bertha rushed to disagree, saying she thought the dialect was marvelously authentic. Listening to this exchange, Ellyn looked as if she would burst into tears at any moment. When Bertha reminded the group that her last Scottish historical romance, *Highland Rapture*, had been number 18 on *The New York Times* extended best-seller list and that she should know whereof she spoke, Jennifer rose a little in her chair and narrowed her eyes.

Eager to avert another battle, Jane stood and asked Larry if he would like to read. He gave her a puzzled look and reminded her that he hadn't written anything new. She apologized, moving on to Carla. Jane had succeeded in preventing another scene. Taking her seat, she glanced at Ivy, who was watching Larry closely.

When the session was over, Adam came in and reminded everyone of the reception he and Rhoda would be hosting in the conference room.

"That's one party I'll pass on," Ivy said softly to Jane.

Jane had no desire to attend either, though she knew she should. She decided to take a few minutes' break in her room first.

She took the back stairs to the second floor and made her way down the corridor.

Passing Arliss's room, she heard Arliss speaking harshly to someone.

"If you want to keep this working," Arliss was saying, exasperation in her tone, "you've at least got to *read* them. Just how lazy are you? You should have told her you're not allowed to talk about them."

What was she talking about, Jane wondered, and to whom was she speaking?

Entering her room, Jane threw herself onto the bed and stared up at the ceiling. Her thoughts wandered to Ivy and Johnny, and she grew angry as she thought about how they had used and manipulated her. She was also certain that Ivy knew more about the gunman incident than she had let on.

Ivy hadn't gone to Adam and Rhoda's reception and must be in her room. Impulsively, Jane decided to speak to her, to confront her about what she'd done.

She crossed the hall and knocked on Ivy's door. There was no answer. Either Ivy had already gone to bed or she was still downstairs, in which case Jane wouldn't want to speak with her now anyway. The things Jane wanted to say could be said only in private. Besides, Jane had decided not to attend the reception; she didn't want to be spotted and buttonholed.

Deciding to speak to Ivy in the morning, she went to bed.

She was awakened by a knock on her door. Morning light shone between the curtains. "Who is it?"

"Jane, it's me, Stanley."

She jumped out of bed, made sure her hair looked all right, and threw open the door. He seemed surprised when she put her arms around him and kissed him. Then she noticed a man in uniform standing behind Stanley, who cleared his throat uncomfortably. "Jane, you remember Officer Raymond."

"Yes, of course," Jane said, serious now, grabbing her robe. "How are you?"

"Fine, ma'am, thank you."

Stanley said, "The road's finally clear, obviously. Now, can you tell me everything you saw relating to this gunman incident?"

"Yes, of course. Let me throw on some clothes."

She closed the door and quickly brushed her teeth and dressed. Then she asked both men to come in and told them what had happened.

"I'd like to speak to Ivy," Stanley said.

"Her room's right across the hall," Jane told him and led the way. Stanley knocked on the door. There was no answer.

"That's odd," Jane said, a shiver of fear running through her. "Where could she be?"

"In another room?" Stanley ventured.

"No . . ." she said thoughtfully. "There's nowhere else she would have spent the night. Stanley," she said suddenly, "I want Adam to let us into her room. What if she's done something — something to herself."

Stanley's eyes widened. "All right." He turned to Officer Raymond. "Dan, would you please go get Adam?"

Raymond nodded and ran down the stairs. A few moments later he and Adam appeared.

"What's going on?" Adam asked Jane.

"I want you to open Ivy's door. She wasn't in her room last night and she doesn't answer the door now."

"All right," Adam said. Taking a ring of keys from his pocket, he unlocked the door and led the way in.

The bed was neatly made, the room empty.

Stanley sighed ominously. "It's clear no one spent the night here."

"Where could she have gone?" Jane asked, though not expecting an answer.

"Jane, I want you to show me where Johnny and the man with the gun ran."

She led them along the corridor, down the stairs, and out the door of the building. It was still quite cold, a moistness in the air, the sky overcast and foreboding. Jane showed Stanley and Raymond the footprints leading into the woods. "But they peter out pretty quickly," she told them.

Stanley was moving slowly among the trees, deeper into the woods. "No, they don't," he said, taking one careful step after another. Raymond, Jane, and Adam followed him. Soon Stanley had led them onto a wide trail.

"Stay to the extreme right, please," he said, "so we don't mess up the prints." He turned to Adam. "Where does this trail lead?"

"To the pond."

"See this?" Stanley said, pointing to the ground. "The prints come out of the woods and onto the trail. And here," he said, pointing along the trail back in the direction of the lodge, "are two more sets of prints. They all merge here."

"But what does that mean?" Jane asked.

Stanley didn't answer, but followed the merged prints, the others close behind. "Ah," he said suddenly, pointing. "Two sets of prints veer off the trail again into the woods."

"Could Johnny and the other man have come this way?" Jane wondered aloud.

"It's possible," Adam said. "Eventually they would have come to another trail. There are so many of them in these woods, and many of them lead all the way down the mountain."

The remaining two sets of footprints continued along the trail, and Stanley, Raymond, Jane, and Adam followed them to the edge of the pond, which was larger than Jane had expected, its surface completely covered with snow.

Stanley walked to the pond's edge, his hands on his hips. He seemed to be staring at something. Jane walked up beside him.

"What?" she asked.

He pointed to an odd mound of snow about a foot from the shore.

"What is it?" she asked, wondering why he found it so interesting. "A rock?"

Wordlessly, Stanley approached the shape, knelt down, and brushed away some of the snow. To Jane's surprise, a bit of bright red was revealed. Puzzled, she frowned and moved closer. Stanley, intent on what he was doing, brushed away more snow.

Suddenly Ivy's face was looking out at them, her blue eyes open, staring, her cheeks bright red.

Jane gasped, stumbling, and clutched at Stanley with a clawed hand. "It's Ivy. Is she . . ."

"Dead."

Jane felt her face contorting and she began to cry. "It can't be. It can't."

Stanley had brushed away more snow. He stood and took Jane in his arms.

Through her tears Jane said, "She must have come down the trail for some reason, not realized she'd reached the pond, and fallen. She must have hit her head on the ice. Poor Ivy."

Gently, Stanley took Jane by the shoulders and looked into her eyes. "Jane, Ivy's death was no accident. I'm sorry, I don't want to have to tell you this, but you might as well know now. She's been stabbed."

Jane's breath caught in her throat. "Stabbed?"

"Yes. With a small, sharp instrument. If I'm not mistaken, an ice pick."

An ice pick . . .

The world began to spin. "Like Trotsky . . ." she said, and suddenly Adam and Rhoda were reaching out to her and calling her name and Stanley had his arms around her again, trying to hold her up, and everything went mercifully black . . . .

112

Chapter Ten

Jane was aware of something cold and hard beneath her. She opened her eyes and saw Stanley's face against the gray sky. His own eyes grew wider, and he smiled with relief.

"Take it easy. Don't try to get up yet."

"What happened?"

"You fainted."

Then it all came rushing back to her — the mound of snow, Ivy's open eyes staring blankly — and she was overcome by a heavy wave of despair.

She felt a drop of water hit her forehead and flinched.

"It's starting to rain," Stanley said. "Do you think you can stand up?"

"I think so."

He took her by the arm, Raymond taking her other arm, and they helped her gently to her feet. "Easy does it," he said. "If you feel faint again, tell me."

"All right." She looked around and saw Adam and Rhoda standing nervously off to the side near a large rock. "Stanley," she said, turning to him imploringly, "what happened to Ivy?"

He paused, clearly reluctant to answer. "I told you, Jane," he said gently, "it looks as if she's been . . . killed." He gave her a curious frowning look. "What was it you said about Trotsky?"

The ice pick. She shuddered. "That's how Leon Trotsky was killed. By an assassin in Mexico City."

Stanley gave her a strange look.

Officer Raymond stepped forward. "Actually, Mrs. Stuart, I believe it was an ice *ax* that was used to kill Trotsky — if you'll forgive my saying so." He gave a quick nervous smile and stepped back again.

Jane looked at him as if he'd lost his mind. "Who the hell cares how Trotsky was killed? My friend is lying there dead on the ice. Who did this to her?" She realized she was screaming. The three men looked alarmed. Rhoda had her index finger between her teeth, her eyes wet with tears.

Now the rain began coming down in earnest, fat plops of water hitting the crusted snow.

"Jane," Stanley said softly, stepping forward, "you've had a very bad shock. I'm going to have Dan here take you back up to the lodge, okay?"

Realizing there was nothing she could do there, that Stanley had to take care of his official business, she took Raymond's arm as he stepped up to her, and slowly he walked her back along the path toward the long wooden building looming ahead.

"Now what happens?" she asked him.

"Detective Greenberg will call dispatch for more officers. Also the Morris County medical examiner. They'll carry out the routine procedures — crime scene — and then," he said, hesitating, "the body will be taken to the autopsy facility."

Wordlessly, Jane nodded. She and Raymond entered the lodge through the door by which they had exited, at the end of the building. Entering the conference room, they stopped short at the sight of everyone sitting around the table, chatting as they ate. A hush descended on the group, puzzled gazes on Jane and the police officer whose arm she was holding.

Ginny stood up. She looked alarmed. "Jane, is something wrong? Where are Adam and Rhoda?"

"Here," came Adam's voice from behind Jane and Raymond. Jane turned. He was picking anxiously at the skin of his thumb. Rhoda stood beside him.

Daniel said, "What happened?"

"Bad news, folks," Raymond said gently, before Jane, Adam, or Rhoda could speak. "There's been a —"

"Ivy's dead," Jane said flatly. "Murdered."

Carla, about to take a bite of buttered poppy-seed bagel, stopped and grinned widely. "I'm loving it."

Everyone looked at her in horror. "Carla!" said Ellyn Bass, who sat beside her.

"Didn't like her," Carla said with a careless shrug, her mouth full of bagel. "That's what she gets for dumping that coffee on me."

"Oh, really," Tamara said.

Jane was aware of movement behind her and turned. Behind Adam and Rhoda were two more uniformed officers, standing side by side. Officer Raymond took a small step forward, taking charge.

"Sir," he said, addressing Adam, "is there a room we can use to interview everyone?"

"Certainly. Through there," Adam replied, pointing toward the lounge.

Raymond stepped to the doorway and took a look into the room. "That'll be fine. If you'll all come in here, please, and take a seat."

"But I'm still eating," Carla protested.

At the other end of the table, Bertha stood suddenly and threw down her crumpled napkin. "Oh, for pity's sake, woman, do as the officer says."

Carla rolled her eyes and flung the rest of her bagel onto her plate. Poppy seeds flew onto the table. "Always so dramatic." But she stood and joined the others, who had already begun filing into the next room.

Bertha stopped when she reached Jane. "How was she killed?" Bertha asked solemnly.

Before Jane could answer, one of the officers stepped forward. "Ma'am, we'd appreciate it if you wouldn't discuss this amongst yourselves."

"Yes, of course," Bertha said with a sharp military nod, and eyed the officer up and down. Jane couldn't help thinking that he was quite handsome — tall, slim, dark-haired, with fine, regular features. Just Bertha's type.

Raymond, who stood close enough to have heard this exchange, spoke to the group. "That's right, folks, no discussion of any sort, please. Officers Bannon and Grady and I are going to take your statements, and then you can get on with your business."

"Get on with our business!" Arliss cried. "I really don't think so."

"Nor do I," Paul Kavanagh said, and there was a chatter of agreement from the others.

"Folks, folks, quiet, please," Raymond said, and turned to Adam. "We won't take up a lot of your time."

Adam said, "That's fine, but they're right. The retreat is over. I assume the old road is plowed, since you're here."

"That's right," Raymond said.

"Then when you're finished with everyone, they can leave?"

"Yes."

Tamara Henley shivered violently. "Then let's get this over with."

The three officers stationed themselves at different spots in the large room, notepads and pens in hand, and began their interviews. It was Officer Grady who spoke with Jane, asking her about her actions and whereabouts since the group reading the previous evening — the last time, it had been ascertained, Ivy had been seen alive. Jane told Grady she had gone directly to her room after the reading. She hadn't attended Adam and Rhoda's reception in the conference room. She had knocked on Ivy's door, wanting to speak to her, but there had been no answer. Then Jane had gone to bed.

When Officer Grady was finished with Jane, most of the others had already given their statements and left the lounge — presumably to pack and leave. Making for the stairway, she passed through the conference room and was suddenly face-to-face with Larry Graham. His skin was shiny with sweat, and there was an odd gleam in his eyes.

"I didn't expect the retreat to end like this."

She frowned. "No, of course not, none of us did. It's a horrible thing. . . ."

"I mean, we were supposed to go through Sunday. If you count today as lost, that's three days we're missing."

Anger welled up inside her, and she gave her head a little toss. "Exactly what is it you want, Mr. Graham? A woman has been killed. How can you be so insensitive?"

He shifted his weight from one leg to the other, opened his mouth, hesitated. Then he said, "I'm sorry about Ivy, but I just meant that because the retreat's been cut short, maybe you could . . . I mean, if I could be in touch with you later on about my manuscript . . ."

She rolled her eyes. "I'm not taking on any new clients at present. I thought I'd made that clear."

"But —"

She swept past him. As she reached the stairway, the outside door opened and Stanley entered. "Are you all right?" he asked.

"Yes, as all right as can be expected. I'm going upstairs to pack."

"I'll come with you."

In her room, she passed him her clothes and other belongings, which he placed in her suitcase on the bed.

"Stanley," she said suddenly, breaking the silence, "who would have wanted to kill Ivy?"

He shook his head. "That's what we're investigating."

"It had to be someone here at the retreat."

"Not necessarily. That fellow with the gun who chased Johnny into the woods managed to get up here."

"But it was most likely one of us. But who . . . and why?"

"We can rule some people out right away. It couldn't have been Adam or Rhoda, because they were hosting their reception in the conference room until after midnight — and it appears pretty certain Ivy died before then. We can also rule out Tom Brockman, because he was also in the conference room the whole time, helping out with the reception."

"What about the people who attended?"

"Can't rule them out. People were drifting in and out all evening, apparently." He took a deep breath. "The prime suspect, obviously, is Johnny."

"*Johnny?* Ivy would have been more likely to kill him." She told him about Johnny and Carla, and about Ivy's reaction. "On the other hand," she said thoughtfully, "they might have argued. The night before last I heard them screaming at each other in their room. What if they fought about Carla, and Johnny lost his temper and killed Ivy?"

"Possible, I suppose," Stanley agreed.

"Damn right it's possible. Ivy told me Johnny used to *hit* her. She showed me a black-and-blue mark on her side."

Stanley looked distressed at this revelation. He looked down, his face reddening, and finally shook his head. "You have to wonder why a woman would stay with a man like that."

"Because she was scared," she said simply. "Scared that if she lost Johnny, she'd have no one."

"And a man who hits you is better than no man at all?"

"To Ivy, yes. She said as much." Tears came to Jane's eyes. "After what happened to Ivy's daughter, Marlene, I'll never forgive myself if Ivy's killer isn't brought to justice."

Stanley's gaze met hers. "Now, Jane, don't you start playing detective again. You're a literary agent. This is a matter for us, the police."

She'd barely heard him. Lost in memories of her long friendship with Ivy Benson, she reached for the last of her clothes and dumped them in her suitcase.

Chapter Eleven

"Missus, what are you doing here? We weren't expecting you and Ivy until Sunday."

Florence stood in the doorway between the foyer and the kitchen, a large bowl of chocolate-chip cookie dough in one arm.

"Hey, Mom —" Nick burst from the family room, his hands full of the miniature soldiers Jane had given him for Christmas. He rushed forward and gave her a tight hug.

She ruffled his clean brown hair, knelt, and planted a kiss on his cheek. "It's good to be home."

He gave her a shrewd look. "But you weren't supposed to be home yet. What's wrong?"

Jane's gaze shifted briefly to Florence, who must also have sensed something amiss and wrinkled her brow. "Is everything all right?" she asked.

"Yes, fine," Jane said brightly. "We ended early, that's all."

Florence was watching her. "Have you had your lunch, missus?"

"I'm not hungry, thanks, Florence.

Maybe just some coffee."

"Of course," Florence said, and went into the kitchen.

Jane hung up her coat and followed her. Nick had returned to the family room, from which came the sounds of *Home Alone*, one of his favorite videos.

Florence came up close to Jane. "What happened?" she whispered. "Where's Ivy?"

"Florence . . ." Jane began, and burst into tears.

"Missus! What is it?"

"Ivy is dead."

Florence's jaw dropped. She set down the bowl on the counter. "Dead?"

"Yes," Jane said, and sniffed.

Florence put a hand to her chest and drew in her breath. "Lord help us, no."

"Yes. Florence," Jane said, her voice breaking, "she was *murdered*." She burst into fresh tears, and the two women embraced tightly.

"But who?" Florence said, patting her back. "Who would want to do that to her?"

"We don't know."

"Poor Ivy," Florence said softly. "I didn't know her very well, but it seems she never had much of a life."

From the center of the laundry room

Jane, Florence, and Nick watched Winky care for her six three-day-old kittens.

"Mom, why can't I play with them?" Nick asked, his gaze fixed on the box in the corner.

"Dr. Singh says we should avoid handling the kittens for the first two weeks," Jane said. "Though I agree it's hard not to at least pet them," she admitted. "They are so cute."

"That they are, missus," Florence said. "But we can name them while we're waiting."

"I've already started on that," Nick said. "Now let's see . . . there are three that look like Winky."

"Right," Florence said. "Brown tortoise-shells. All females."

"Right. But they don't look exactly alike. One has funny dark marks above her eyes that look like another pair of eyes. So I've decided to call her . . . Four Eyes."

"Sounds good," Jane said, and she and Florence exchanged a smile.

"Then there's one with dark paws. I'm calling her Muddy, because it looks like she stepped in mud. And there's one that looks exactly like Winky. I haven't figured out what to call her yet."

"We'll work on that one," Florence said.

"What about the other three?"

"There's that gorgeous one with the grayish-white markings," Jane said.

"Also a tortoiseshell," Florence said. "I believe it's called a blue-cream."

"How do you know so much about cats?"

"I told you, missus, in Trinidad I saw a lot of kittens being born. Now this blue-cream tortoiseshell, it is also a girl."

"Let's call her Blue," Nick said.

"Okay," Jane said. "Now what about the other two?"

"Ah, the boys," Florence said. "And both orange tabbies."

"They're beautiful," Jane said, looking at the tiny orange-and-cream striped bodies. "What about these guys, Nick?"

"Well," he said thoughtfully, "one is more orange than the other, and I've noticed he keeps stomping on his brother and sisters. So I think we should call him Crush. Get it? Orange Crush."

"Love it. And the other one?"

"He's the smallest of the litter. He's Pee Wee."

"Very good, Master Nick," Florence said, and tossed back her head and laughed. "You still have to give some thought to the one that looks just like her mother."

"I will." Nick frowned in puzzlement. "Why are they all different?"

"Genetics," Jane said. "Not that I can explain it, but nature dictates that a certain mother and father will produce certain types of kittens."

"You know," Florence said thoughtfully, watching Winky, "I have read that a litter of kittens can have more than one father."

Jane looked at Florence in shock.

"It's true. While you were at the retreat, I thought about who the father might be — you know, tomcats in this neighborhood. And there are *two* I can think of who might be responsible for this bunch. I even called Dr. Singh, and she told me what this is called." Florence glanced upward, thinking. "Yes, I know. Superfecundation."

"Wow. You're smart, Flo."

Florence patted Nick's head. "No, just curious."

"Look what she's doing now."

Winky moved around the box, rubbing heads with each of her kittens in turn. Then she walked to a corner of the box and flopped onto her back. Immediately the kittens made their way over to her and began to nurse.

"You're a good mother, Miss Winky," Florence called softly, and she and Jane and Nick filed quietly out of the room.

"Hey, Mom," Nick said in the hallway. "Do you think Ivy would like to have one of the kittens?"

Jane's and Florence's smiles disappeared. Jane opened her mouth but was at a loss for words. Finally she said, "Nicholas, honey, I have something to tell you about Ivy. During the retreat" — she glanced quickly at Florence — "she had an accident."

"An accident? Is she all right?"

Jane put her hand on the back of Nick's head. "No, darling, she's not. I'm afraid she died."

Nick's face grew pale. "What happened?"

"She . . . fell on some ice and . . . hurt herself. I'm so sorry to have to tell you this news."

"Dead," Nick said hollowly, and caught his lower lip between his teeth, contemplating this idea. "And she was just here, having Christmas with us."

"Yes," Florence said, "that's right. And we had a lovely Christmas, didn't we? I'm sure Ivy left this world with happy thoughts in her head."

The two women watched Nick walk slowly down the hallway to the foyer and

128

enter the family room; then they exchanged a sorrowful look. A tear rolled down Florence's cheek and she wiped it away, forcing a little smile.

Early that afternoon, Stanley called before dropping by. Jane made hot cocoa and served it with some of Florence's chocolate-chip cookies in her study off the living room.

"Are you sure you're all right?" he asked.

"I'm fine, really. It's just a terrible shock. She was my oldest friend."

"I know." He placed his hand on top of hers. "I want you to know we're working very hard on this, Jane. I'm sure we'll have some answers soon."

"Why do you say that? Have you got any leads?"

He looked uncomfortable. "No, not exactly. There were no fingerprints of any use at the crime scene, as you would probably have guessed. The ME says Ivy didn't put up a struggle. That means the killer sneaked up on her."

"No, not necessarily," Jane said impatiently. "She and the killer could have been chatting, and the killer could have whipped out that awful thing and stabbed her."

"I suppose," Stanley said, "but not very

likely, in my opinion."

She shrugged. "Could the medical examiner tell from the wound whether the killer was right- or left-handed?"

He gave her an appraising look, lifting one brow. "Quite the detective, aren't you? Actually, I was going to tell you about that next. Unfortunately, in this case he wasn't able to tell."

She let out a sigh of discouragement. "Then I don't see why you're so confident about having answers soon. It looks as if this case may never be solved."

"Of course you're feeling negative about everything now. . . ."

"Someone needs to," she cried. "Poor Ivy, without a friend in the world."

"You were her friend," he pointed out softly.

"Not a very good friend. After Marlene died, I was happy to let the friendship be over. I should have gotten back in touch with her, tried to patch things up. It shouldn't have had to be Ivy who put our friendship back together. I feel so guilty about it all."

He sat silently for a moment, sipping his cocoa.

"I'm sorry," she said, smiling at him. "I don't mean to dump all this on you. What else can you tell me?"

"The footprints were pretty quickly washed away by the rain, but we did ascertain that there were *five* sets of prints, not four as we originally thought."

"Five?"

"Mm. Here's how we think it went down. Two people — presumably Johnny and his pursuer, the man with the gun — ran through the woods, onto the path for a short distance, then back into the woods. *Three* people, not two, followed the path from the lodge to the pond. Only two of these people, obviously, came back: the murderer and . . . someone else."

"Who could this other person have been?"

"Unfortunately, the prints were obliterated enough that trying to match them with the shoes of the people staying at the lodge was impossible." He set down his cup. "In the meantime, I've got some men searching the woods for signs of Johnny and the gunman."

Jane set down her cocoa and sat staring into the middle distance, contemplating this information. At this moment she felt that Johnny was the likeliest suspect in Ivy's murder, yet he himself had been another's quarry. Why had that man wanted

Johnny? Where was Johnny now?

Aware of Stanley rising from his chair, she came out of her reverie.

"I should go," he said.

"I'm sorry, I haven't been very good company."

He bent and gave her a kiss on the cheek. "Don't worry about it. Try to get some rest. I'll be back tomorrow."

She saw him to the door and watched him back out of the driveway and head down Lilac Way.

Chapter Twelve

After seeing Stanley off, Jane had returned to her study and tried to get through a stack of book proposals that had been submitted to the agency before Christmas. But it was hopeless. She couldn't concentrate. Letting a handful of pages drop to her lap, she gazed aimlessly out the window, which looked out on the left side of her smallish front yard, the high holly hedge that enclosed it, and Lilac Way beyond.

As she watched, a car pulled slowly up the street and slowed when it reached Jane's house. The car was white, with familiar lettering on the side. It pulled into Jane's driveway, and she realized it was a Shady Hills Taxi.

Frowning in bewilderment, she went to the front door, opened it, and looked out. Behind the wheel of the cab, eighty-something Erol, who had been driving for Shady Hills Taxi for more than thirty years, saw Jane, grinned, and saluted. She smiled and waved back, then squinted, straining to see who his passenger was. All she could make out were moving shadows as whoever it was in the back paid Erol, he handed back change, and the passenger handed back some money, presumably a tip. Erol looked at the bills he'd been handed and scowled.

The right rear door of the taxi opened, and an immense bouquet — no, two bouquets — of red and yellow roses emerged first.

What on earth . . . ?

After the roses came a pair of pudgy legs.

No. It couldn't be.

It was.

With difficulty, Bertha Stumpf extricated herself from the cab. She pulled down her tight dress with a shimmying movement, then slammed the car door shut. Erol backed out and drove away up the street.

Bertha looked appraisingly up at the house, eyes narrowed. Then she saw Jane, her face bloomed into a solicitous smile, and she started up the path to the front door.

What was she doing here?

"Surprise!" Bertha cried, clip-clopping up the steps in her heels. "Bet I'm the last person you expected to see, huh?"

"That's for sure." Jane made herself smile. It occurred to her that she should have seen this visit coming. Over the course of their working together, Bertha had made several references to the possibility of their getting together sometime "in Jane's neck of the woods." Jane had found the idea repugnant. Not only did she find Bertha tiresome at the best of times, but she never socialized with the writers she represented. Even if she did, the last thing she would ever do would be to invite one to her home.

Years ago, when Jane and Kenneth had both worked at Silver and Payne, the large old literary agency where they had met, Beryl Patrice, the agency's president, had given Jane a piece of advice: "Don't ever wear your mink to lunch with a client, and whatever you do, don't ever let a client see where you live. Either the client will feel you live too lavishly and have achieved this affluence off her back, or else the client will feel you live shabbily and will decide you're a loser. Either way, it causes resentment. It's a no-win situation."

It was the only thing of any value Beryl had ever said to Jane. She wondered which category Bertha would fall into.

"Jane, darling!" Bertha cried dramatically, bearing the vivid bouquets up the steps like an Olympic torch, and threw her arms around Jane. "Please forgive my dropping in like this, but how could I leave town without knowing you were all right?"

"How did you know where I live?"

"You're in the book, Jane." Bertha trotted past Jane into the foyer. "What a fabulous house. So old-fashioned and cozy. And so big! What do you call this style?"

"Chalet, mock Tudor." Jane shrugged. Was this really happening?

"Well, it's adorable. Here," Bertha said, practically shoving the flowers in Jane's face. "These are for you, darling. I figured you could use some cheering up after what happened this morning. I'm so sorry." Jane took the flowers, and Bertha shrugged out of her coat.

Florence and Nick appeared from the kitchen and stood staring. "Bertha — oh, sorry," Jane said.

"No, my real name is fine here, silly," Bertha said with a wave of her hand. "This is family."

Family. Hanging up Bertha's coat, Jane felt as if she were going to be sick. "Bertha Stumpf, I'd like you to meet my son, Nicholas, and this is Florence."

Nick said a quick hi. Florence looked bewildered at this unexpected guest but stepped forward graciously and shook Bertha's hand. "A pleasure to meet you," she said.

Bertha gasped. "*Love* the accent," she said, as if it were something Florence had selected and purchased. She gave Florence and Nick an arch smile. "I've heard a lot about you two."

Still they both stood there, staring. Jane gave Florence a quick wave of her head that meant *Beat it.*

Florence relieved Jane of the roses, then took Nick by the hand and led him back toward the kitchen.

"My word," Bertha said, watching Nick nostalgically. "Such a handsome young man. The spitting image of Kenneth."

Bertha had known Kenneth in the early years when she and Jane worked together, but she was wrong about Nick's looks. In actuality, Nick looked mostly like Jane. But Jane felt no desire to point this out to Bertha, who now stood in the center of the foyer, looking around. "Well."

"Well is right," Jane said, able to bear it no longer. "Bertha, what are you doing here?"

Bertha turned to her, shock on her face. "I just told you. I wanted to make sure you were all right before I left town. How could I leave without seeing you?"

Easily, Jane thought.

"I mean," Bertha went on, "what's the difference whether I take a later bus? You matter most. So," she said, and turned a piercing look on Jane, "how're you holding up?"

"As well as can be expected." Anger welled in Jane and though she tried, she couldn't keep it tamped down. "Bertha, this really is the height of insensitivity. My oldest friend died last night — was murdered — and you use her death as an excuse to stop by here, at my home, to talk about your career."

Bertha opened her mouth as wide as it would go. "My *career?* What are you talking about? I've just told you twice —"

"Yeah, yeah, you told me twice. And you're full of it twice. I know you better than that."

"What are you saying? That I'm not a thoughtful person? Who was it who saved your life that time at the Waldorf when you were hurt so badly? Who told the police and the EMTs who you were? Who came to the hospital to make sure you were all right?" Bertha's eyes were moist with tears. "Really, Jane, I'm very hurt."

Jane rolled her eyes. "All right, I'm sorry. You want some coffee?"

"I'd love some," Bertha said, immediately back to business, and roamed into the family room. "Fabulous house," she marveled. "Fabulous."

"This way," Jane said, and led her into the living room.

"Even more beautiful," Bertha pronounced as she arranged herself comfortably on a sofa.

"I'll be right back," Jane said, and went to the kitchen.

"Missus," Florence whispered as soon as she saw Jane, "who is that woman?"

"Yeah, Mom," Nick said from the kitchen table. "She's so fat."

"Nicholas! That's a terrible, unkind thing to say."

Nick shrugged. "I can tell you don't like her."

She stared at him. "What do you mean by that?"

"I can tell, that's all. I can always tell. I think it's called body language."

"Oh, really?" Jane said, unable to suppress a smirk. "And what kind of body language was I using with her?"

"The kind that says, 'I don't like you, but I'm going to pretend I do.' "

Florence giggled. "Missus, can I make you and your friend some coffee?"

139

"Thank you, Florence, that would be lovely. And some of those cookies if there are any left." Jane glanced at Nick's crumb-covered plate. "And by the way, she's one of my clients. She writes romance novels under the pseudonym Rhonda Redmond."

"Ah," Florence said, her face lighting up, "the very successful Rhonda Redmond."

"Right," Jane said, "so behave yourselves, both of you."

Nick let out an evil little snicker, and Florence gave one solemn nod. Jane returned to the living room, where Bertha sat with her legs crossed. "Jane, I feel I'm intruding."

Very perceptive. "No, don't be silly, Bertha. It's a surprise, that's all. Perhaps if you had called first . . ." *I would have had a chance to tell you not to come.*

"You're right, I should have. But I didn't have your home number."

"Yes, you did. You just said I'm in the book."

"Oh, yes, right." Bertha shifted uneasily. "Anyway, I'm here now, and as soon as I'm sure you're all right and that there's nothing I can do for you, I'll be on my merry way."

"Very thoughtful," Jane said, sitting on

the sofa perpendicular to Bertha's. "I'm fine, really."

"It's all such a shame. Not only about your friend, but about the retreat. It was going so well, don't you think?"

Jane frowned. "No, as a matter of fact, I don't. No one got along. Everyone was constantly sniping at one another. And the students' work itself was extremely disappointing — except, maybe, for William Ives's novel. I thought that was remarkably well written."

Bertha rolled her eyes and gave a lazy wave. "Please. Do you really think he wrote that? Gimme a break. Arliss wrote it for him."

"I know that's what Brad Franklin said, but do you really think so?"

"Absolutely. It was of publishable quality. How could that dried-up little raisin of a man have written that himself?"

"What does his appearance have to do with how he writes? You're not exactly — forgive me — Marilyn Monroe." *On the other hand, you're a lousy writer, so maybe you've got something there.*

"No, no, that's not what I meant. It's just that he came out of nowhere."

"You came out of nowhere once."

Bertha made an exasperated *tsk*ing

sound. "Anyway, he wasn't the only student whose work had merit. My own Ellyn Bass is a lovely writer."

"You think?"

"Definitely. She writes with genuine passion. That's all that really matters. When you write with passion, your readers know it. Why do you think I'm so successful?"

"I don't know, why are you?"

Bertha placed the palms of her hands to each side of her on the sofa. "Jane, you are angry at me for coming here. Don't deny it. Instead of making these passive-aggressive little quips, why don't you speak your mind? I'll be happy to leave if you like. I'm not staying long anyway."

Jane lowered her gaze, duly abashed. "I apologize, Bertha. You're right. I was annoyed to see you. I never have clients in my home, and I'm not exactly in a visiting mood."

"All right, then. Thank you. Let's start again, shall we?"

Florence came in with the coffee and cookies. "Here we are," she said, and set them down on the cocktail table.

Bertha put milk and Equal in her coffee and grabbed two cookies, munching on one as she watched Florence leave the room. "She's a treasure, isn't she?"

"Yes, she is. She's like family."

"Like I said," Bertha cried in a high-pitched voice. "Me too. And what kind of relative would I be if I hadn't stopped by? So we were talking about the retreat and that sweet Ellyn Bass. You keep an eye on her, Jane. She may very well be the next me."

Heaven forbid. "Thanks for the tip. She is a member of the writers' group here in town, the Midnight Writers, so I can keep tabs on her."

"Good." Bertha started on her second cookie. "Have you heard from your friend Stanley?" she said with her mouth full. "Does he have any idea who did that awful thing to Ivy?"

"No. It's soon yet."

"True. But we all know who did it, don't we?"

"Who?"

"That Johnny, of course. I can imagine exactly what happened. I'm not a novelist for nothing, you know." Bertha closed her eyes and threw back her head theatrically. "Ivy was mad for the man," she began in a husky voice that reminded Jane of Norma Desmond in *Sunset Boulevard*. "And what happens? He and Carla take one look at each other and a fiery passion rages." She shook her head sadly. "Ivy had no hope of keeping him, poor little thing. But love doesn't die without a fight. On the path down by the pond, she confronted him, told him she loved him, demanded that he forget Carla . . ."

Jane remembered the sounds of shouting that came from Ivy and Johnny's room.

Bertha swept on, "But he would have none of it! He told her they were through. She slapped him. He hit her back. He has a furious temper — men like that always do. Enraged, she slapped him again. They struggled. She wouldn't let him go. And Johnny knew that the only way he could ever have Carla was to get Ivy out of the picture. So he whipped out the ice pick and —" She let her head fall. "Well. You know the rest."

Jane stared at her in amazement. " 'He whipped out the ice pick'? What would he be doing carrying around an ice pick?"

"I don't know." Clearly Bertha felt this was a triviality. "He'd put it in his pocket earlier — you know, without thinking."

"Oh, Bertha," Jane said, "that's ridiculous. Whoever killed Ivy stole that ice pick with the express intention of using it on her later. This was no crime of passion."

"Hmm," Bertha said, considering, and shrugged. "Then I have no idea. *Unless*," she burst out suddenly, "it was Carla! She wanted Johnny for herself and had to get Ivy out of the way. Now that would make more sense."

"Yes," Jane had to admit, "it would." Then she had another idea. "You know, I've just remembered something. On Wednesday night Ivy told me Red Pearson had made two passes at her. She wasn't at all interested, of course. Maybe —"

"Maybe Red killed Ivy because she wouldn't have him? No way."

"How can you be so sure?"

Bertha blushed. "Because," she said, placing a hand delicately to her bosom, "Red Pearson was interested in *me*."

"In you?" Jane faltered.

Bertha stared at her coldly. "Is that so unbelievable?"

"No, no. It's just that I had no idea."

"C'est vrai," Bertha said airily, then hunkered down. "I think he's dishy, don't you?"

"Red? Bald Red Pearson in the red flannel lumberjack shirts? Uh, no, I don't."

"Wait till you're a bit older, Jane. You won't be able to be so choosy."

"I won't need to be. I'll have Stanley."

"And if he loses his hair? Will you lose interest?"

"No."

"All right then. It may very well be that Red was interested in Ivy at the beginning of the retreat, but that was before he got to know me." Bertha wiggled her eyebrows. "And boy, did he get to know me."

"Bertha! There are some things I don't need to know." But Jane marveled that she hadn't been aware of this particular situation.

"And there *are* things you don't know," Bertha said, as if reading her mind. "Anyhoo, that's where I was after the police let us leave the lodge this morning — at Red's house. He's got a darling place way up at the north end of town — not terribly far from Mt. Munsee, actually — with the prettiest little yard —"

"You went to Red's?" Jane asked, scandalized.

"For *lunch*. We had a lovely time, and we're going to be getting together again, probably in New York. It was while I was at Red's house that I had the idea of stopping by to see you before I left town. Red wanted to drive me here, but I knew he was eager to start on some project in his house and told him I wouldn't dream of it.

146

He had to get to some store called the Depot, or something like that."

"Home Depot."

"That's it. He said he hadn't expected to be home from the retreat so soon, but now that he was, he might as well get started. Your house would have been far out of his way. So he called me a taxi."

"I see," Jane said, growing bored. She wanted Bertha to leave now. She set down her coffee cup and stifled a yawn.

"You're exhausted, poor thing. I should go. Lord knows I need to get back to my desk. Lots to do."

"Oh?" Jane said, and the moment the word was out of her mouth she realized she'd fallen into Bertha's trap.

"Absolutely. Now that Harriet's accepted *Shady Lady* — you're checking on my money, don't forget — I've got to get started on a new proposal. The question is, who is it for?"

"What do you mean, who is it for? It's for Bantam, your publisher."

Bertha looked directly into Jane's eyes. "I can't stay there, Jane. As I've told you, I can't work with this girl they've assigned to me, and you said there's no one else there to work with."

"Whoa, hold it, whoa. What I said was

that Harriet Green is a fine editor. I never said there's no one else at Bantam you could work with. What I said was that Harriet was as good an editor as any editor there."

"I find that difficult to believe. She's twelve!"

"Bertha, I've told you how that bothers me. It's ageist and disrespectful. She's a young woman. How would you like it if she called you a senior citizen? And what difference does it make how old she is? A good editor is a good editor."

"Jane, you have to understand about my writing, about me. I write romance from a worldly, experienced perspective. I bring my life wisdom to my writing. I can't communicate with a woman barely out of college. She doesn't understand where I'm coming from."

"Baloney."

Bertha stared at her. "I beg your pardon?"

"Baloney. Nonsense. Fact is, many of your readers are Harriet's age. If you think you're not getting through to them, you're in trouble."

"I take it, then, that you are not willing to ask that I be assigned to a new editor."

"You take it correctly. There would be no point."

"Then I must leave Bantam."

"Leave Bantam?" Jane cried. "You've been there most of your career."

"Exactly. Time for a change. My print runs are declining, and so are my sell-throughs. I don't make the printed *New York Times* list anymore. I don't even get a step-back cover anymore," she said, referring to a double paperback cover.

"Bertha," Jane said as gently as possible, "none of these problems have anything to do with Bantam. You won't reverse these trends unless you change what you're writing."

"Change what I'm writing! Rhonda Redmond?"

"Rhonda Redmond whose print runs and sell-throughs are dropping. We've talked about how the market for historical romances is changing. Why don't you try a Regency historical? That's what's hot right now."

"Regency," Bertha repeated distastefully. "So mannered and polite. Hardly a fitting backdrop for a Rhonda Redmond heroine."

"But that's just the point." Jane felt a headache coming on. "A Rhonda Redmond heroine would be all the more shocking and scandalous in that society."

"Mm," Bertha said, though she was clearly uninterested. She brushed off her dress and rose. "I really should be going, Jane. Now that I know you're all right."

"And we've discussed your career."

"Oh, my goodness," Bertha said with a surprised little laugh. "We have, haven't we."

"But we've resolved nothing."

"True, but I do appreciate your thoughts, as always. You want me to write a Regency historical for Harriet at Bantam."

"Yes."

"Let me give it some thought." Bertha started toward the foyer. "Now if you'd be a doll and call me a cab to take me to the bus . . ."

"Don't be silly. I'll drive you," Jane said, taking their coats from the closet.

"You would? You're a sweetheart. Oh, and Jane . . ." Bertha said, buttoning her coat.

"Yes?"

"Please don't tell anyone about Red and me — not that you would, of course."

"Right. I wouldn't."

"Thanks. You know how people are."

Yes, Jane thought, putting on her scarf, she knew how people were. And as she headed for the kitchen to tell Florence and Nick she'd be right back, it occurred to Jane that she should be grateful to Bertha. She had, at least for a time, managed to take Jane's mind off poor Ivy.

Outside, Bertha paused and gazed up at the house. "Nice place," she said with a thoughtful frown, and started along the path to Jane's car.

Chapter Thirteen

It was 9:30 P.M. Jane, Florence, and Nick had just checked on Winky and her brood — Winky had now taken to vigorously licking her young, which Nick found hilarious — and then Jane had gotten Nick into the shower and tucked into bed. Now, standing at her dresser and removing her earrings, she heard the doorbell ring.

Florence's steps sounded in the hall. "I'll get it, missus. I wonder who . . . ?" After a moment there came the sound of the front door opening, and Florence's voice again, "Why, Mr. Daniel. Are you okay?"

Daniel? Jane went out into the hall and to the edge of the stairs. Daniel, in jeans and coat, gazed up at her, a look of concern on his face, his brows drawn together.

"Hi, Jane. Sorry to bother you so late."

She descended the stairs. "What's wrong?" Reaching the foyer, she took him by the arm and led him through the living room into her study. It wasn't like him to simply show up, especially late in the evening.

"Jane," he said, taking the same seat

Stanley had occupied earlier in the day, "something's been bothering me, something that happened yesterday at the lodge. I felt I should tell you about it, see if you thought it was worth mentioning to Stanley."

"Go on."

He shrugged off his jacket and laid it down on the small table between their chairs. "It was late yesterday morning, about eleven o'clock. Ginny had asked me to help set up for lunch. She realized the supply of napkins in the kitchen had run out, so she sent me to get some in that storage room off the lounge."

She nodded encouragingly.

He went on, "It took me a minute or two to find the napkins — it's quite a mess in there." He made a face. Messes always bothered Daniel. "Finally I found them and was about to leave the storage room, but as I was about to open the door, I heard voices in the lounge and realized they belonged to Larry Graham and Ivy."

Jane gave a bewildered little shrug. "So?"

"It was the *way* they were talking. I sensed something odd right away, and I confess" — he looked down in embarrassment — "I peeked out a crack in the door and watched them. They were sitting extremely close together on the sofa, and their heads were practically touching. Larry was smiling, and Ivy was leaning toward him, pressing her body against him. She said something like, '. . . down the path. It's safe there,' and Larry nodded, very serious."

" 'Down the path'?" Jane sat up straight.

"Yes."

"Then what happened?"

"At that moment a noise came from the conference room beyond them — it sounded like someone bumping into a chair. Ivy and Larry both looked up sharply, and then Larry ran out to the conference room. He came back a few moments later. He told Ivy he'd heard footsteps on the stairs and had run up to see who it was, but that there was no one in the upstairs corridor, that whoever it was must have gone into his or her room." He stopped, watching her, waiting for her reaction.

"How positively odd," she said. "Were Ivy and Larry going to meet on the path? What could she have meant when she said it would be safe there?"

Daniel shook his head, at a loss.

Jane said, "Do you think Ivy and Larry could have been carrying on at the same time as Johnny and Carla?"

"Larry was hardly Ivy's type," Daniel pointed out.

"True, but she may have been using him to get back at Johnny." She suddenly remembered Ivy watching Larry so intently during the group reading Thursday evening. Could she have been planning her revenge on Johnny at that moment?

"I see why you thought this was so important," she told him. "What if Ivy and Larry did meet," she said thoughtfully, "Larry made clumsy advances toward Ivy — maybe wanted to go further than she wanted to — and she rebuffed him?"

"And he killed her in a rage?"

She shook her head. "Why would he have been carrying the ice pick?" She paused, thinking. "Our Larry theory doesn't really make sense, but I think we'd better tell Stanley about this. Why haven't you said something sooner?"

"I don't know. . . . In all the uproar, I guess I forgot. Then I remembered it, and it occurred to me that it might very well have significance."

"It may not, but the police have to know about it." She rose, picking up Daniel's coat and handing it to him. "Let's go."

Stanley lived on the top floor of a house on Christopher Street, not far from Hillmont Elementary, where Nick attended the fifth grade. From his La-Z-Boy in the corner of his small plant-filled living room, he listened to the end of Daniel's story and slowly nodded.

Jane said, "We don't know if it's significant, but we felt you should know about it."

"Absolutely. I know this Larry Graham character. The town had some trouble with him a couple of years ago."

"Trouble?" Daniel repeated.

"Mm. He bid on the electrical part of that big library renovation and got the job. But halfway into it, he claimed he'd been lied to about the original electrical work in the building and needed twice the money to do the job right. Not only did the library board feel that this was blackmail, but they couldn't understand why he hadn't inspected the building carefully enough before he started to know this. They weren't even sure they believed him anyway."

"So what happened?"

"The board refused. They offered him a payment for what he'd done. He took it and stomped off, wouldn't cooperate with the new electrician they brought in. On top of that, it was discovered that he'd been cutting corners, and everything he did had to be ripped out. The board considered suing him, but in the end they decided not to throw good money after bad." Stanley shook his head. "Totally sleazy character."

"Are you going to speak to him about him and Ivy?" Jane asked.

"Absolutely. First thing in the morning." He shot Jane a warning look. "Now don't *you* get any ideas about playing detective and speaking to him."

Jane placed her fingers to her throat, affronted. "I wouldn't dream of it."

"Good," Stanley said, and gave a decisive nod. "I'll let you know what I come up with."

The next morning, Saturday, Stanley stopped by to see Jane. She was in the kitchen, making breakfast for Nick, who was in the laundry room watching Winky and her kittens. Stanley sat at the kitchen table and Jane gave him some coffee.

"I've just been to see Larry Graham," he said.

Jane turned, a bowl of beaten eggs in her hand. "And?"

"What a sleazy jerk."

She laughed. "Very professional."

"I'm not speaking as a police officer, of course."

"Of course."

"Anyway, he was shocked when I asked him about his intimate conversation with Ivy. He wanted to know how I knew about it. I didn't tell him, of course. He admitted to having the conversation and confirmed that Ivy said, '. . . down the path. It's safe there.' But guess what he said they were talking about."

She waited.

"Ice skating."

"Ice skating?"

"Mm-hm. You're not going to believe this, but fat, pasty-faced Larry is a former professional figure skater. Roughly twenty-five years ago, of course."

"You're right — I don't believe it."

"It's true. He says he had told Ivy all about it, and she wanted him to skate for her."

"How ridiculous. Even if he really was a skater, he wouldn't have had skates with him at the retreat. Besides, the pond was covered with snow."

"I put both those facts to him. He said they had agreed to borrow a snow shovel

158

from the storage room and clear some of the pond. And he did have skates with him — at least he said he did."

"Why would he have brought skates?"

"Because he knew there was a pond near the lodge and thought he might skate there."

She poured the eggs into a hot frying pan and they sizzled. "He's full of it. I hope you didn't believe him."

"No, I didn't. Though I can't imagine why he wouldn't have just admitted that he and Ivy were planning to meet down the path to fool around."

"Because of Johnny, of course. He would have been afraid of what Johnny would do to him."

"Good point," he said. "I think they were planning to meet down the path because there was nowhere else they could meet — there weren't any rooms available, and they weren't going to use the storage room, after the fuss you said Tom Brockman made. I think Larry wanted more than Ivy was willing to give, and he got angry and killed her."

"With the ice pick he'd pilfered from the lodge's kitchen." She gave him a skeptical look. "Why would he have done that?"

He contemplated his coffee mug. "I have

159

no idea," he said, deflated.

"Are you sure he's telling the truth about this skating stuff?"

"His mantel is lined with trophies and photos. I intend to check on it, of course — a search on the Internet should do it." He sipped his coffee. "But I'm not really interested in this Graham character. I don't intend to pursue him further at this point. It's Johnny Baglieri I'm after. I've still got men searching Mt. Munsee for signs of him and the guy who was chasing him. The ME says Ivy died between eight P.M. and midnight Thursday night. Johnny could have escaped his pursuer — or dealt with him in a worse way — and returned to the woods near the lodge to take care of Ivy."

"But why? What reason would he have had?"

"Maybe simply that she knew too much about his life, his dealings, his 'irons in the fire.' Who knows what he's involved in."

"But why would he have chosen to do it then?" She shook her head vehemently. "It doesn't make sense."

The eggs were ready. She scraped them from the pan onto a plate, which she placed at Nick's seat, then started making toast. "Nick," she called. "Breakfast."

He appeared in the doorway almost instantly, as if he'd been waiting in the next room.

"Mom," he said excitedly, slipping onto a chair. "I thought of a name for the kitten that looks just like Winky."

Jane and Stanley waited, watching him.

His face broke into a huge smile. "Twinky."

Stanley smiled. *"Twinky?"*

"Yup," Nick said solemnly. "It's short for 'tiny Winky.' Get it?"

Nodding, Jane threw Stanley a conspiratorial look.

"Know what else?" Nick said on a mouthful of scrambled eggs. "She's the one I'm keeping."

Stanley looked up in surprise. "You're keeping one of the kittens?"

"Yes, just one," Jane said, and looked at Nick. He was looking down sadly. She walked around the table and put her arm around his small shoulders. "We discussed it and agreed that one was as much as we can handle."

"Right," Nick agreed halfheartedly. "I hope Winky doesn't miss her other children too much."

Stanley gave him a kind smile. "I'm sure she knows your mom will find them good

161

homes. Right, Jane?"

"Right," Jane said, looking down at her son, and squeezed him tight. "That's a promise."

After Stanley left, Jane went to her study to give the proposals another try. She rejected two and was halfway into her third when her thoughts drifted to what Stanley had told her about Larry Graham. She tried to picture him, obese and ungainly, spinning on ice, but the image was just too comical to take seriously. But, of course, as Stanley had pointed out, Graham had looked quite different in his skating years. . . .

The telephone rang. It was Daniel.

"Any news?"

She told him what Stanley had told her about Larry Graham.

"A skater? Him? That's the funniest thing I've ever heard."

"Mm, ludicrous, isn't it? But apparently it's true. . . ."

"Why do you say it like that?" he asked suspiciously.

"Because there's more there than what Stanley got; I'm sure of it. And I intend to find out what it is."

"Now, Jane . . . What are you going to do?"

"I'm going to go see Graham myself. And don't you dare tell Stanley. I'm sick of his lectures about not playing detective."

"I won't. But you don't know where Graham lives."

"Not a problem. Talk to you later."

"Jane —"

She hung up. Then she thought for a moment and took the phone off the hook.

She yanked out the telephone directory from the bottom drawer of her desk and checked the Yellow Pages under Electrical Contractors. Larry (not Lawrence) Graham was listed, but there was no street address, just "Shady Hills Area." His listing in the White Pages was the same.

Adam would know the address. She got his number from her address book and punched it out.

Chapter Fourteen

Larry Graham lived at Hillside Gardens, a vast but down-at-the-heel apartment complex at the east end of town, across Route 46. Jane found a parking space not far from number 78, Graham's apartment. Graham opened the door before she could ring the bell. He wore jeans and a faded yellow T-shirt.

He looked her up and down in slack-jawed amazement. "What are you doing here?"

"I'm surprised to find you home," she said pleasantly. "Such a beautiful day." It was indeed a lovely day, sunny and unseasonably mild, the snow turning to slush. "I would have thought you'd have jobs to go to."

He laughed derisively. "Jobs! Why would I have any jobs today? I didn't line anything up. I was supposed to be at the retreat until tomorrow."

He actually sounded as if it was Jane's fault that Ivy had been murdered, spoiling his week.

"Good point," she said. "May I come in?"

He regarded her suspiciously. "What do you want?"

"I'd like to talk to you," she said, forcing her tone to remain gracious and keeping a mild smile on her face. She glanced into the apartment. "Well, may I?"

He shrugged indifferently. "I guess so."

She couldn't remember when she'd last been in an apartment like this. Everything about it was dingy, from the filthy gold-colored plush carpet that appeared to run through the entire place, to the scuffed off-white walls. The air had an oppressive animal stench, bringing to mind a large unwashed dog — which was exactly what appeared from the rear doorway of the living room. Jane didn't know much about dogs, but she knew this to be a collie. Its pale-gold-and-white coat was matted and dull; its eyes were a rheumy blue.

"Don't mind Alphonse," Graham said, flopping into a chair and indicating the sofa for Jane. It was as dirty as the carpet, but she made herself sit anyway, keeping her coat on. The dog hurried up to her and buried its nose in her lap.

"How sweet," she said, squirming. "But I'm afraid I may be allergic," she lied. "Could you call him off, please?"

"Alphonse!" Graham screamed, and

Jane jumped. "Leave 'er alone."

The dog immediately withdrew its nose, slunk to the corner of the room, and fell onto its side, tucking its nose into its tail. It made a few snorting noises and closed its eyes for a nap.

Jane looked around the room. To her right was a fireplace, whose mantel was indeed lined with an assortment of skating trophies in various sizes. She spotted a picture of Larry skating in a pure white costume. He looked slim and athletic, not unattractive. Shifting her glance to Larry — pudgy, ungainly, the very picture of ungracefulness — she found it barely possible to believe.

He followed her gaze. "Yeah, it's true," he said. "I suppose your boyfriend told you about that part of my life."

"Why do you say he's my boyfriend?"

"Who?"

She felt herself blush. "Never mind."

"So let's cut the small talk, shall we? You're not here because you think I'm the next John Grisham. To what do I owe the honor?"

She realized she found him loathsome. Ivy couldn't possibly have been interested in him romantically. "I want to ask you about something."

He rolled his eyes. "My conversation with your friend? Listen, I'm sorry about what happened to her, I really am, but I don't know anything about it."

"What did she say to you?"

"Like I told Greenberg, she wanted me to skate for her. We agreed we'd meet down the path at the pond."

"At night."

"In the evening. It's never totally dark up there on the mountain. When else could I have skated for her?" he whined. "The retreat went all day."

"And you'd brought your skates with you to the retreat?"

"Yeah, *like I told Greenberg,* I knew there was a pond up there. I still skate a lot." His gaze shifted to Alphonse, now quietly snoring.

Graham was lying, Jane was sure of it. Though there was no way Ivy would have been interested in him, he might very well have been interested in Ivy, and Ivy might have intended to use that interest to her own advantage. "You can tell me if you and Ivy were going down the path for . . . to . . ."

"Make out?" His mouth opened wide in a mirthless laugh. His belly shook. "With her? Baby, I may not be what I once was, but I'm not that hard up."

"What's that supposed to mean?"

"Your friend, if you'll forgive me, wasn't exactly my type. Been around the block, if you know what I mean. Besides, she was Johnny's girlfriend. And nobody was going to cross Johnny — at least, nobody with any brains. And brains is somethin' I pride myself on havin'."

"Not your type, eh?" Defensiveness for her poor dead friend rose in Jane like a tangible wave. "And what are you, Cary Grant?"

"Hey! You want to insult me, you can get outta here."

"I'm sorry, I'm sorry," she lied. "Please forgive me. I don't know if you're aware of this, but Ivy was my oldest friend. We went to college together; we were roommates. I'm trying to figure out what happened to her, who did that to her."

"Why don't you leave that to the police?"

He sounded like Stanley. "I'm . . . helping the police," she said evenly. "Now. You say Ivy wanted to see you skate. So she convinced you that it was safe —"

"On the ice," he said, nodding vigorously. "So we agreed to meet that night at the pond. Simple as that."

"Mm," she said, trying desperately to think of another tack. Then, all at once, she had it. "By the way, I've been thinking about your thriller idea — you know, about the bus hijacking."

He sat up a little. "Yeah?" He scowled suspiciously. "I thought you said you weren't takin' on any new clients *at present*," he mimicked her.

"That's my standard line." She winked at him. "You understand. Otherwise I'd be inundated with submissions. But I've been thinking about your project, and I think you've got a smashing idea for a novel. You know, straight out of today's headlines." *Lord forgive me.*

His eyes widened and he raised his ginger-colored brows. "So you think it could go somewhere?"

Yeah, right into the reject pile. "Definitely. I have to tell you quite honestly that I was disappointed that you didn't write more during the retreat. I saw promise in your writing."

"You did?"

"Yes, I did."

He sat back and smiled. "Well, what do you know. Hey, that's great. So you think if I, you know, worked up more of the project, maybe you'd, like, work with me on it. Represent me?"

"Almost a certainty. Of course, I'd need a full outline of the story and at least the first three chapters. But I think I can say even at this point that it's a project I could really get behind."

His entire expression changed, growing warm and animated. "This is great news. You know, I always knew I had it in me, all these years I been sloggin' away as an electrician. I always knew I had what it takes. 'Larry boy,' I'd say, 'you did it with skating, you can do it with writing.' Hey, an artist is an artist, right?"

"Absolutely." She shifted on the dirty sofa. Then she waited, smiling at him.

He studied her for a moment, then leaned forward in his chair. "Uh, listen, Jane. Now that we're going to be working together, I guess I can be straight with you about what happened up there. Your friend Ivy — she was some kinky chick."

"What do you mean?"

"Well, she was playing some kind of weird game with me. Okay, I admit it, she had a thing for me, and I thought she was kind of foxy, in a slutty kind of way."

Jane forced her smile to remain in place.

He went on, "At first I didn't dare take her up on her advances because of Johnny.

Finally I told her that. She laughed and said she and Johnny were finished, that Johnny was only interested in Carla. So I relaxed a little."

"What did you mean about a 'weird game'?"

"You're not going to believe this, but because I was writing a thriller about the bus hijacking, she thought *I* was the hijacker!"

"You?"

Alphonse jumped, then snuggled his nose back into his tail.

"Yeah. Funny, isn't it?" Graham said.

"But why did she think that?"

He smiled with only one side of his mouth. "Because she thought I knew that the hijacker's briefcase bomb wasn't real before it broke in the news. Fact is, I heard it on the radio like everybody else."

She remembered Ivy, sitting on her bed Wednesday night, asking if Jane had heard any more about the hijacking story.

"At least, she *pretended* to believe I was the hijacker," he continued. "So I went along with it, played her game. I figured, 'This babe is hot for me and gets off on this kind of make-believe stuff, so what do I care?' So anyway, that conversation in the lounge — it was about the money she

171

thought I'd gotten in the hijacking."

"The money?"

"Yeah. She was pretending to blackmail me. She said she'd expose me if I didn't give her money. She wanted to meet me down by the pond to talk about it." He winked at her. "But I knew what she really wanted."

Jane winked back, feeling as if she might be sick at any moment. "Gotcha. And did you meet her?"

He looked down, embarrassed. "Nah. I thought about it all afternoon and decided it was a dumb idea. Not worth it, you know? She could *say* Johnny wasn't interested in her anymore, that he wanted Carla now, but how did I know if she was right about that? What if she was just using me to make Johnny jealous? Like I said, I wasn't about to make Mr. Johnny the Wiseguy mad."

"So if you didn't meet Ivy down the path, where were you that night?"

"In my room. I told that to your boyfriend."

Inwardly she winced. "Right. Did you tell him any of this?"

"No. Didn't think he'd understand." He sat up. "You believe me, right? I mean, you don't think I killed your friend?

'Cause I got an alibi."

"You do?"

"Sure. Ives."

"William Ives?"

"He was my roommate. He was in the room with me all Thursday night. You can ask him. He'll vouch for me."

"Of course he will. If you don't mind, I think I will speak with him, just as a formality. You wouldn't happen to know where he lives?"

"Sure I do. It's not far from here. He lives with his granddaughter. I'll get you the address. Ives and me, we got pretty chummy up there. Nice old guy. We promised we'd get together for a drink or somethin' once in a while, talk books." Laboriously he lifted himself from his chair and crossed the room to a console table next to where Alphonse still slept. He picked up a slip of paper from the table, grabbed another piece of paper and a pen, and jotted something down. "Here you go," he said, handing the paper to Jane. "Tell him I said hi. And you have my permission to tell him you and I'll be workin' together."

"Let's not jump the gun," she said hastily. "First things first."

"Oh, right. An outline and three chapters. Gimme a couple days."

"You got it," she said, rising, and was pursued all the way to the door by Alphonse, whose nose she could feel pressing into the back of her thigh.

William Ives lived about a quarter of a mile from Hillside Gardens, in one of the smallest houses Jane had ever seen. Getting out of the car, she reflected that it was barely more than a shack, a box covered with shingles shedding their coat of wine-colored paint, and topped with a deteriorating roof. A few scraggly juniper bushes lined a flagstone path up to the screen door, behind which stood shriveled William Ives himself, watching Jane with a puzzled look.

"Hello, Mr. Ives," she said cheerfully, approaching the door.

He made no response.

"Bet you're surprised to see me."

"My granddaughter's at work," he said, as a child might say his mommy's not home.

"Yes, I know you live with her. May I speak to you for a moment?"

"Sure," he said, but didn't invite her in. "That check I gave Adam for the retreat come back or something?" he asked, his thin voice rising nervously.

She laughed. "No, I'm sure it didn't. I just want to ask you a question. I'm terribly sorry to bother you and won't take up more than a minute of your time."

"A question?"

"Yes, an easy one. Was Larry Graham in your room with you on Thursday night?"

"Thursday night?" He frowned. "How am I supposed to remember that?"

"It would be extremely helpful if you could. Thursday night was, of course, the night before Ivy Benson's body was found."

The dry wrinkles between William's eyes drew together. "You think Larry did it?"

"I didn't say that," she responded evenly. "I'm just asking you a question. Was Larry with you the entire evening?"

His body shifted behind the screen door. "Why are you asking me about this? You're not the police. Unless your detective friend put you up to it."

"Actually," she said, feigning embarrassment, "he did. I help him out from time to time."

"I see," he said, and paused. Finally he said, "As a matter of fact, Larry was with me all that night. I know because we played blackjack the whole time. He beat

175

me bad. I still owe him."

She regarded him through the door, tiny and shrunken in brown corduroy pants and a hooded red sweatshirt. He looked back at her, his thin lips set firmly. She believed he was lying. Why she believed this, she couldn't say.

"Mr. Ives, do you know it's a crime to lie to the police?"

"But you're *not* the police!" he said, and let out an ugly cackle. "Besides, I'm not lying. Why would I lie?"

He narrowed one eye. "Listen, if you're smart, you'll go talk to that vamp, Carla. Everyone saw how she and Johnny were carrying on. Carla and Ivy probably had an argument about him, and Carla killed Ivy. Simple. And you know that Carla has a mean temper. You saw how mad she got when Ivy dropped that coffee in her lap."

Suddenly he turned and looked back into the house. "I hear my great-granddaughter. She's up from her nap. Now leave us alone!"

And he shut the door in her face.

Chapter Fifteen

It was noon when Jane pulled into the parking lot of the Shady Hills Diner on Route 46. It occurred to her that Florence, who had agreed to watch Nick, might be wondering where she was, so she called home on her cell phone. Nick answered. He and Florence were having lunch. The big news was that Winky, who hadn't ventured much out of the laundry room since giving birth, had just made a brief appearance in the kitchen.

Entering the diner, Jane found herself face-to-face with a glass case of revolving pies — Mississippi mud and lemon meringue and gooey, glistening pecan. It occurred to her that something sickeningly sweet would feel very good right now, after the upset of the past few days; but she fought this urge, knowing that such an indulgence would only succeed in putting back some of the weight she'd recently lost.

"One?" the hostess asked her.

"Yes," Jane replied, wrenching her gaze from the pies. "Is Carla here?"

"Carla? Sure, she's right over there." The hostess pointed.

Carla stood at a large table, taking an order. She wore a tight pale-blue uniform. Her ash-blond hair, still parted in the middle, was pulled back into a tight bun, accentuating her beak of a nose. At that moment she glanced up and saw Jane; she registered no emotion and immediately returned her gaze to her order pad.

"I need to speak with her," Jane said.

The woman frowned. "Well, as you can see, she's on duty. I can sit you at one of her tables if you like."

"Yes, that would work. Thank you."

The hostess seated Jane at a table for two only a few feet from where Carla stood. Carla was just finishing taking the orders from the occupants of the large table. Turning, she stepped directly over to Jane's table, as if she'd seen her sit down with eyes in the back of her head.

"Why do I get the feeling you're not here for a cheeseburger deluxe?"

"Hello, Carla."

Carla waited, pad and pen in hand.

"I would like a cheeseburger deluxe, actually. But cheddar, please, not American. With a Diet Coke. I'd also like to talk to you."

"Can't. I'm on duty."

"Carla, speak to me or speak to the cops. I'm told I should be speaking to you about Ivy's murder."

With a sudden smooth movement Carla slipped into the chair facing Jane's and leaned forward. "Listen, Jessica Fletcher, I know exactly what you're thinking. I would have liked nothing better than to kill Ivy when she spilled that coffee on me. But I'm no murderer." She gave a self-satisfied little smirk. "And I certainly don't need to commit murder to get the guys I want."

"Quite the mantrap, aren't you?" Jane said, moving her head suavely from side to side, mocking Carla's smug tone.

Carla sat up, embarrassed. "So are you gonna get out of here, or what?"

Jane frowned in shock. "Get out of here? You haven't even brought me my lunch. Now, as I was saying, if you want to avoid getting a visit from a member of the Shady Hills Police Department, you'd better talk to me. It won't take long."

Carla waited.

Jane said, "All I want to know is what you were doing Thursday night — the night Ivy was killed."

Carla threw out her hands. "I was doing

179

lots of stuff. I can't give you a minute-by-minute."

"Let me put it another way, then. Did you see Ivy that night?"

Carla pursed her lips, thought for a moment, then let out an exasperated sigh. "I saw Ivy twice, both times *inside* the lodge."

Jane waited.

Carla said, "The first time was in the lounge. I was blabbing with Vick Halleran, Tamara Henley, and that gross slob Larry Graham. Did you know he was once a figure skater?"

"Yes," Jane replied impatiently. "Go on."

"At the other end of the room, Ivy was talking to Bertha Stumpf — or Rhonda Redmond, I should say — and Jennifer Castaneda. I heard Jennifer say she was going outside for a cigarette, and Ivy said she'd join her. Jennifer was wearing this big thick sweater — you know, like a fisherman's knit — so she didn't need a coat or anything. But she told Ivy she'd freeze in the thin red sweater she was wearing. Ivy gave her a wave of her hand and said it didn't matter, she'd be fine, and they left together. I saw them go outside through the reception room door. Not too long after that, Vick excused himself to me, Tamara, and Larry, and left too."

Jane nodded encouragingly.

"I realized I was bored out of my mind talking with these people. Tamara is such a snob, and Larry — well, he gives the word *sleazy* new meaning. So I made up a reason to get out of there. Actually, I had a real reason. The room I was sharing with Ellyn had been freezing cold all day, so I went out to the reception room to complain to Adam about it.

"While I was talking to Adam, Ivy and Jennifer came back into the lodge. That was the second time I saw Ivy. Jennifer had been right about Ivy getting cold, because now Ivy was wearing Jennifer's white sweater. They were laughing about how much better the sweater had looked on Jennifer. Which is true — that broad's got some bod, let me tell ya.

"Ivy and Jennifer went into the lounge. I finished telling Adam to fix our heat and followed the two of them in. I was relieved to see that Larry was gone. Unfortunately, Tamara was still there, and Vick had come back."

"He'd come back?"

"Mm. And I noticed that he looked . . . kind of uncomfortable to see Jennifer come in. Everybody knew they were fighting a lot. Vick must have hoped he'd gotten rid of her for a while. Anyway, I didn't want to get stuck talking to him and Tamara again, so I grabbed some book from one of the shelves and sat down alone to read it. But wouldn't you know, Tamara came right over to me and asked me if I wanted to rejoin her and Vick. She said they were having a very interesting discussion about the public's current taste in literature. Can you imagine? I told her I'd rather read. I think I pissed her off, because she didn't answer and just turned, said good-bye to Vick, and walked out of the room."

"Then what did you do?"

"Nothing — I kept reading. The book wasn't bad, actually. Ivy and Jennifer had sat down together and were still joking around about how Ivy looked wearing Jennifer's sweater. Ivy took off the sweater and gave it back to Jennifer. Then Ivy said she was tired and was going up to her room. She left the lounge, and that was the last time I ever saw her."

"What did you do for the rest of the evening?"

Carla rolled her eyes in frustration. "After a while I went to my room, where I was stuck talking to the terminally boring Ellyn. But I didn't want to go out again. I stayed in the room for the rest of the night."

Carla stood. "Now get out."

"Probably a good idea," Jane said, casting a sickly look at a passing tray of food, "but one last question first."

Carla waited, shifting her weight from one hip to the other.

"Have you seen Johnny since he ran out of the lodge?"

Carla stared at her, poker-faced. "No."

"You're lying."

Carla leaned down close to Jane's face. "Listen, Mrs. Smarty Pants Literary Agent, I'm not answering any more of your questions. Now get out of here before I ask the owner to call the police."

"Call them," Jane said pleasantly.

"Oh, that's right, that Greenberg guy's your squeeze. Well, I haven't seen Johnny, okay? I don't know what happened to him. Is that so hard to believe?"

"Yes."

"Why?"

"Because of how much you were attracted to each other."

"It happens." She shrugged. "You saw the guy with the gun. Johnny may be dead, for all I know."

"We can only hope," Jane said, rising,

and walked out of the diner.

As soon as she had shut the car door, she whipped out a pad of paper and a pen and made notes about what Carla had told her. Then she drove home.

She found Florence and Nick in the laundry room, where they seemed to spend most of their time these days, watching Winky and her six kittens.

"Mom, look what Winky's doing," Nick said, pointing, a look of dismay on his face.

Winky had picked up Crush, the larger of the orange tabbies, by the scruff of his neck. She carried him across the box and set him down. Then she picked up Crush's younger brother, the other orange tabby named Pee Wee, and did the same to him.

"Ouch. Why is she doing that?"

"It doesn't hurt them," Florence assured him. "Mother cats do it all the time."

They watched as Winky flopped onto her side to nurse.

Florence turned to Jane. "And how are you doing, missus?" she asked quietly. "Are you all right?"

"Yes . . . just very sad. And curious."

Florence gave her an inquiring look.

"Thanks for watching Nick," Jane said, then went to her study, where she took out

184

her notes from her conversation with Carla Santino.

One detail seemed relevant. Larry Graham was gone when Ivy returned to the lounge with Jennifer. What if, instead of going to his room as he'd told Stanley and Jane he'd done, Larry *had* gone down the path to meet Ivy after all. Ivy, obviously, had not gone to *her* room.

Jane stared pensively out the window.

Making a decision, she returned to the laundry room and asked Florence to keep an eye on Nick again. Then she hurried back to her car, pulled out of the garage, and drove quickly down Lilac Way.

Chapter Sixteen

"You back already?" Graham said in surprise. "I'm already workin' on those chapters, but I'll need more time than this." He laughed, amused by his own joke.

"I'm not here about your book. May I come in, please?"

"Yeah, sure." He opened the screen door. Alphonse immediately appeared and pressed his cold nose against Jane's knee. She walked into the smelly living room, the dog in close pursuit. She turned to Graham with an imploring look.

"Alphonse," Graham shouted, "get outta here."

With a high-pitched whine, the dog turned and walked out of the room.

Jane sat down on the sofa. Graham stood in front of his chair. "Well?"

"Mr. Graham," she said, readying herself for her bluff, "someone saw you walking down the path to the pond on Thursday night. I know you didn't really go straight to your room. Why did you lie? What really happened?"

He sat down in the chair, watching her

appraisingly. "Who says they saw me?"

"I can't tell you that."

He paused, eyeing her warily, and finally spoke. "I'm not sure I believe you, but I'll tell you the truth anyway. I did go to my room from the lounge, and I stayed there for a little while, but I got to thinking about Ivy and . . . well, you know . . . she started lookin' better and better."

"Even though she might have been using you to make Johnny jealous?"

"I guess I was willing to take my chances. I was —"

"Horny?"

He looked horrified, embarrassed beyond words. "Anyway, like I was sayin', I decided to go meet her, play along with her weird game about me bein' that bus hijacker. She'd asked me to meet her down the path at nine o'clock, so a few minutes before nine I slipped out of the lodge and went down the path to the end, at the edge of the pond."

"And?"

"And she wasn't there. I waited a few minutes, no longer than that. Then I decided she wasn't coming. But as I was starting to leave, I saw her lying near the edge of the pond. I went close and saw she'd been stabbed with the ice pick." He wiped his hand across his glistening forehead. "I totally freaked out. I ran back to the lodge. I went in by the door to the kitchen and hurried up to my room."

He looked down. "I made a deal with old William. If he would say I was in our room the whole night, I'd do whatever electrical work needed to be done in that dumpy shack of a house he and his granddaughter live in."

"I see," Jane said slowly. "Did William want to know why you needed such an alibi?"

"Yeah, he asked. I told him Ivy and I had had a big fight, that Ivy was really upset, and that I didn't want to get in trouble with Johnny. He bought it. The old creep."

"Why do you call him that?"

Graham sat up straighter, frowning in outrage. "The next day, after they found Ivy's body, he came up to me and said now he knew the real reason why I needed him to say I was in the room all night. He said electrical work wasn't going to be enough, not by a long shot."

"What did he want?"

"I didn't give him a chance to get to that. I told him I couldn't talk about it then, that I'd be in touch to work things out."

"Then you intended to give him more?"

He threw out his hands. "Sure I intended to give him more. What else was I supposed to do? How would it look if the police knew I'd left my room the night Ivy was murdered? They'd pin it on me so fast your head would spin."

"But if you're innocent . . ."

"Are you for real? What does that have to do with it? Lady, in this country, innocent people end up behind bars, and guilty people walk. Happens every day. Ain't you heard about O.J. Simpson, Claus von Bulow . . ."

"Von Bulow was acquitted."

This information appeared to make no difference to him.

"I wasn't about to be part of that crowd."

"I see." She rose.

"What are you going to do now?"

"I'm going to tell Detective Greenberg what you've told me. If you're innocent, as you say you are, then you have nothing to worry about."

"So who saw me?"

"I'm sorry, I'm not at liberty to tell you that."

From her car she called Stanley on her

cell phone and told him what Graham had said. Stanley said he would be right out to talk with Graham again, adding, "I'm still not sure I believe a word he says."

Jane drove to the ramshackle little house where William Ives lived with his granddaughter and great-granddaughter. This time it was Ives's granddaughter who answered the door. She was a tired-looking, big-boned blonde. She gave Jane a cautious once-over. "Yes?"

"My name is Jane Stuart. I'd like to speak to your grandfather, please."

"Gramps," the woman called back into the darkness of the house. "There's a woman named Jane Stuart here to talk to you."

For several moments the two women stood staring at each other. Finally Ives appeared, taking hold of the front door and letting out an irritated sigh when he saw her. "You back?"

"Yes. I want to ask you something. I've just been speaking to Larry Graham, and he told me about an interesting arrangement the two of you had."

The old man's eyes widened, then flashed to his granddaughter. "Roseanne, I'll be fine."

Roseanne shrugged and walked back into the house.

"What 'arrangement'?" Ives asked.

"I know about the payment you wanted for not telling anyone Larry Graham wasn't in the room with you all night Thursday. You know that's blackmail."

He bristled. "What business is this of yours?"

"Ivy was my best friend. How she died is my business."

"We don't know that Larry did it."

"No, but he's afraid the police will think he did, and you took advantage of that."

"So what?"

She shook her head. "I just wanted to verify that this 'arrangement' had taken place. Good-bye."

She walked back to her car, called Stanley again on her cell phone, and told him the part of Graham's story about the blackmail was true.

"Thank you, Jane. I appreciate your help," he said, but there was an odd stiffness in his tone. She decided to ignore it.

"Also," she went on, "I've been meaning to ask you. Is Johnny's car still parked up at the lodge?"

There was a brief silence. "Yes, actually, it is. We're going to impound it. If you must know, the car was stolen. It's been traced to a woman in New York City."

"Not surprising," she said. "He grabbed a car and got out of there."

"Mm," he said.

"Stanley, what's wrong? Why do you sound so odd?"

She heard him exhale, as if trying to control himself. "Jane, I appreciate your help, but you can stop playing cop now, stop interviewing people. In fact, I want you to stop. The chief said something to me today. Apparently William Ives called and complained about you bothering him."

Why, that little weasel.

Jane heaved a great sigh of impatience. "Look, Stanley. I've been running around getting you information you weren't able to get — information you've been only too happy to follow up on — and all of a sudden you want me to stop 'playing cop' because someone complains that I paid him a courteous visit. I never even went into his house, for Pete's sake."

"Jane, I'm only saying —"

"You can tell your chief that I will continue to try to find out who killed my friend Ivy. This is America; you can't control me like that. This is *my personal business*. Besides, judging from the way you and your colleagues have been handling the case, I don't have much confidence you'll solve it."

He was silent on the line.

"Good-bye, Stanley."

"Good-bye, Jane."

She snapped her cell phone shut and shook her head. Then, gazing out the window at Ives's shack of a house, she thought about the path, about the third person who went down to the pond Thursday night. The murderer. She decided that the likeliest suspects, after Johnny, were Larry and Carla.

Larry had wanted Ivy, that was clear. They might very well have fought. In a rage Larry might have stabbed her. But why would he have had the ice pick with him?

Carla had wanted Ivy's man. The two women might also have had a fight that culminated in murder. Jane thought Carla had been lying when she said she hadn't seen Johnny since he fled the lodge. How could Jane check up on Carla?

Of course. Ellyn Bass.

Jane called Adam. Rhoda answered.

"Hi, babe." Rhoda's tone was deeply sympathetic. "How are you holding up?"

"I'm okay, Rhoda, thanks. I still can't believe it."

"Has Stanley found out anything? Any leads?"

"No, not yet. Rhoda, is Adam there?"

"No, he had to run some errands. You want me to have him call you?"

"Maybe you can help me. I need Ellyn Bass's address."

"Sure, hold on." Rhoda put down the phone and came back on a moment later. "Here it is. Sixty-three McCoy Drive, Lincoln Park."

Jane thanked her and hung up. She started the car and headed north. Less than ten minutes later she had reached Lincoln Park. She pulled into a gas station and got directions to McCoy Drive.

It was a curving street in an affluent development consisting of large modern homes on smallish, carefully landscaped lots. Ellyn Bass's house was a taupe raised ranch. Jane approached the front door on a paving-stone path that ran between rows of low, bare azaleas. A few feet from the walk, near the front steps, a tricycle lay on its side. Not far from the tricycle was a small orange ball and a naked Barbie doll.

Jane rang the bell. From behind the door came the sound of a child running; then the knob jiggled. Finally the door opened, Ellyn Bass gently pulling away one of her

194

twins, a pretty little girl with an abundance of dark hair.

"Mrs. Stuart!" Ellyn burst into a warm smile. "I can't believe you're here. How are you?"

"I'm fine, thank you, Ellyn. And please call me Jane. I hope you don't mind my stopping by like this."

"Don't be silly. It's wonderful to see you." Ellyn frowned sympathetically. "I'm so sorry about your friend."

"Thank you," Jane said graciously.

"Come in, come in." Ellen pulled the door all the way open, and Jane stepped into a spacious two-story foyer with a sweeping, curved staircase. In a corner of the foyer stood a magnificently decorated Christmas tree that reached the ceiling of the second floor.

Jane followed Ellyn into the living room. On a cream-colored carpet sat expensive cinnamon-colored leather furniture and glass-and-iron tables. "What a lovely home you have."

"Thanks. Coffee?"

"No, thanks. I can't stay long."

Looking curious, Ellyn sat down on the sectional sofa, and Jane sat too. At that moment the little girl who had come to the door raced into the room, followed by a second, identical little girl. Ellyn regarded them with dismay.

"Alyssa, Breanna, why don't you go back to the TV room and watch your *Little Mermaid* video?"

The girls ran out of the room. Ellyn dropped her shoulders in relief. "Now," she said, smiling sweetly, "what can I help you with?" She rolled her eyes upward in an expression of modesty. "I'm sure it's not about the romance I'm writing."

"No, I'm afraid it's not. Ellyn, I want to talk to you about Carla."

"Carla?" Ellyn's brow creased in puzzlement.

"I need to know if Carla was with you in your room the night Ivy Benson was killed — Thursday night."

Ellyn's eyes widened. "You think — you think Carla —"

"I don't think anything," Jane said hastily. "I'm asking this about everyone. I'm . . . helping the police, you might say."

"I see. Hmmm." Ellyn nibbled the inside of her lower lip, thinking. Suddenly her face reddened. "To be honest with you, she did kind of slip out at one point."

" 'Kind of slip out'?"

"She left."

"When? Do you recall?"

"I'd say a little before nine o'clock. But I know where she went," Ellyn said quickly. "She went to see Johnny."

"Really?"

"Yes. The reason I know is that earlier that day, during writing time, Carla and I were in our room when suddenly Johnny knocked on the sliders from the balcony. I nearly had a heart attack."

"What did you and Carla do?"

"She let him in, of course. They acted as if I wasn't even there." Ellyn looked down, a hurt expression on her small face. "They arranged to meet that night. I promised Carla to keep their meeting a secret — she didn't want Ivy to find out about it and, you know, make a stink — but of course this was before poor Ivy got murdered. All bets are off, right?"

"Absolutely. Where were they going to meet?"

"They were going to 'meet' " — Ellyn made quotation marks in the air — "in Johnny's car. Pretty tacky, huh?"

"I'll say — though I'm not surprised."

"Me neither," Ellyn said. "I hate to say this, but Carla is not a nice person. In fact, I'd say she's downright vicious."

"Vicious?"

"Yes. Do you know, on Wednesday night

she was undressing for bed and I happened to see that her thighs were burned from the coffee Ivy accidentally spilled on her. I said something about the burns, that maybe she should get a doctor to look at them. She completely ignored me. Her eyes turned into little slits, as if she was reliving the whole thing, and suddenly she blurted out — please pardon my French — 'I'd like to kill that bitch!' "

"That certainly qualifies as vicious," Jane said. "Is there anything else you can remember that might be . . . pertinent?"

"No, I don't think so." Ellyn leaned forward. "Do you think Carla might actually have killed Ivy?"

"I don't think anything at this point. We're only gathering information." Jane stood. "Thank you, Ellyn, you've been extremely helpful."

"My pleasure," Ellyn said, walking Jane to the door. "I hope you'll think about doing another retreat. I had such a wonderful time. I honestly felt that someday I might achieve something with my writing."

"You will achieve something if you don't give up," Jane said sincerely. "As for another retreat, I can't say at this point."

"Of course you can't. I understand."

"Mommy, Mommy!" One of the twins

appeared in the living room, her tights down around her ankles. "I had a mistake."

Ellyn threw her a weary look. It wasn't difficult to see why she had enjoyed the retreat.

"I'll let you get on with your day. Thanks again," Jane said to Ellyn, who was already tending to Alyssa/Breanna's mistake, and went out the door and made her way down the path to her car.

Heading back toward Shady Hills, Jane wondered if Ellyn's sleazy account of Carla and Johnny's tryst was true, or if Ellyn could possibly have been covering for Carla as William Ives had tried to cover for Larry Graham. Ellyn might even have added that last bit about Carla's rage to *appear* to be protecting her. Then Jane decided this was too far-fetched, that this theory didn't fit Ellyn's personality. What reason would she have had to protect Carla?

Ellyn was right: Carla was vicious. Jane was reluctant to approach her again, though of course she had to.

In the meantime, she wished she could find and speak to Johnny, who she now knew hadn't fled Mt. Munsee as early as everyone believed.

Chapter Seventeen

As Saturday evening approached, Jane wondered if Stanley would call. They almost always went out for dinner and a movie on Saturday night.

But he was no doubt mad at her. Remembering what he'd said to her made her even angrier at him. She wasn't sure she wanted to see him. . . . No, she did want to see him, and decided to call. From her study, she punched out his home number.

He sounded deeply relieved to hear from her. "I'm sorry about what I said."

"Thank you, Stanley, but I believe I need to apologize to you."

"For what?"

"For embarrassing you in front of the chief. I'm sorry."

"So you've decided not to play detective anymore?"

"I didn't say that. What I mean is, I'm sorry I have to do what I'm doing."

"*Why* do you have to do this?" he said in a tone of forced patience.

"Because Ivy was my best friend, first of all. And because sometimes I think, well, that the police need some help."

"Okay, fair enough. So you're going to go on 'helping' us, but you regret that you have to do it."

"Yeah, that's about right."

He laughed. "Well, I know I couldn't stop you anyway. In fact, I don't believe I'd be able to stop you from doing anything you intended to do. But do me one favor?"

"Sure, name it."

"Keep me out of it."

"Really?" she asked, surprised. "In the past you've made good use of my help."

"And gotten in trouble for it."

"Stanley, you didn't get in trouble for solving cases with my help; you got in trouble for involving me in police business. What a bunch of hypocrites you all are."

"Yes, that we can be," he said brightly. "Now, what are our plans tonight?"

She smiled. "I'd love to see that new Russell Crowe movie. And we still haven't tried the new Greek place in Parsippany."

"It's a date."

It was strange to be with Stanley but not discuss Ivy or what Jane had learned that day. But Jane had a good time nevertheless. They talked about their plans for New Year's Eve, which was only two days away, and decided on a quiet evening at Jane's house — dinner with Nick (and Florence, if she didn't have other plans), a rented video, and champagne while they watched the ball drop in Times Square.

She knew for sure that she and Stanley were back on good terms when he kissed her deeply at the door before she went in.

Late Sunday morning Jane fortified herself and drove to the Shady Hills Diner. The hostess, the same woman who had seated Jane the day before, was puzzled to see her again. Perhaps she had witnessed the unfriendly exchange between the two women.

Carla, she said, was off today. Jane asked for Carla's home address.

"I'm sorry, I can't give you that," the woman said, no doubt curious as to why, if Jane was her friend, she didn't know it.

"No prob," Jane said, figuring she could always get it from Adam if she had to.

Then she got an idea. She went to the ladies' room, and on the way, stopped a waitress hurrying in the other direction. "Excuse me, I'm a friend of Carla Santino's from California. I didn't realize she wasn't working today. She doesn't know I'm here — I want to surprise her. I just found out she moved. Do you happen to know her new address?"

The woman, who wore a name tag that read *Jean*, frowned. "Carla didn't move. Hey, Bernie," she hollered to a man behind the counter. "Carla's still at Heather Gardens, right?"

"Far as I know."

"Oh, she's still there," Jane said. "I don't know where I got the idea she'd moved. Would you happen to know the apartment number offhand? I don't think I have it in my book."

"What number, Bernie?" Jean asked.

Bernie rolled his eyes, then turned and consulted a handwritten list on the wall. "Sixty-seven."

"Great," Jane said. "Thank you so much."

Heather Gardens was a condominium complex not far down the road from Hillside Gardens, where Larry Graham lived. In fact, the two complexes were practically identical. Jane parked in front of number 67, walked up to the scuffed tan front door, and rang the bell.

After a moment the door opened, and Carla stood there in a skimpy Hawaiian-print wrap, her ashy hair in a ponytail. Jane noticed that she wore no makeup. Her face had a dry, haggard look.

For the briefest moment Carla stared at Jane, her face expressionless. Then she slammed the door.

"Why, that —" Jane moved closer to the door. "Carla, I need to speak with you. Please. I know you met with Johnny on Thursday night. If you won't talk to me about it, I'll have no choice but to ask the police to do it."

After a moment the door swung slowly open. Carla regarded her furiously. "Well, come in."

Jane stepped into a tiny vestibule. Carla apparently had no intention of letting her go any farther into her home. "Well, what about it?" she demanded.

"Why didn't you tell me you'd met with Johnny?"

"What are you, stupid? Why do you think? Because I was afraid to."

"Afraid? Why?"

Carla nervously fingered a gold chain around her neck. "Because if you or the police knew Johnny was still around that night, you might think he killed Ivy — which he didn't. Or, if you knew I wasn't really in my room all night, you might think *I* did it." Through slitted eyes she gave Jane a sidelong glance. "How'd you find out I saw Johnny?"

Jane had no intention of putting Ellyn on Carla's bad side. "Let's just say you were seen. Are you still in touch with Johnny? Are you going to see him again?"

"I'm . . . in contact with him," Carla answered cagily. "I have no idea if we'll get together again." She cast her eyes heavenward, recalling pleasure. "Though I'd sure like to."

Jane regarded Carla thoughtfully. "Listen. I need to speak to Johnny. I'll make a deal with you. If you tell me how to reach him, I'll keep your meeting on Thursday night a secret."

"A little blackmail. Okay," Carla said slowly. "I guess he won't mind my giving you his number. He's a big boy. Wait here." She disappeared into the apartment for a few moments, then reappeared with a slip of paper on which a phone number was written. She handed the paper to Jane and smirked. "Tell him to call me."

It was a New York City number, area code 212. For a brief moment, Jane considered sharing it with Stanley, then remembered their conversation and decided against it. Besides, she always accomplished more on her own.

In her car, she called the number on her cell phone. The phone rang four times and was picked up by an answering machine. "Leave a message," came Johnny's rough-edged voice.

"Johnny, it's Jane, Jane Stuart. I need to see you. It's urgent." She left her cell phone number, not wanting him to call her at home.

She was back in her neighborhood, driving along Grange Road, when her cell phone rang. She pulled over and answered it.

"What do you want?" Johnny asked without preamble. He sounded different now — brusque, tougher.

"I know you were still around the lodge when Ivy was murdered."

"Murdered!"

Was he really surprised? Wouldn't Carla have told him?

"Yes, I'm afraid so," she replied, playing along. "The police are looking for you as the prime suspect. You can talk to them or me."

"You. Here in Manhattan. Tomorrow morning."

"Fine. Where?"

"In the park."

"Central Park?"

"Yeah. Uh . . . there's this playground. Go into the park at East Seventy-ninth Street."

"All right. What time?"

"I don't know, ten. And listen to me, Jane. You go to the cops about me, you're gonna be one very sorry lady."

Chapter Eighteen

Jane got out of the cab at 79th and Madison and checked her watch. It was ten minutes before ten. She started walking the block to Fifth Avenue. The weather had turned fiercely cold — the temperature wasn't expected to rise above 23 degrees all day — and a relentless wind whipped between the stolid rows of townhouses, blowing back Jane's hair and finding its way up her sleeves and down the throat of her heavy wool coat.

Head lowered against the wind, she crossed Fifth Avenue and entered the park. Ahead lay the playground, deserted, as she'd expected it to be. To her right stood a row of benches, and she sat down on the one nearest to her, crossing her arms in front of her for warmth and surveying the icy gray landscape. At the horizon, black silhouettes of the skeletons of trees shook violently, as if they might break at any moment. As she watched, a dark figure detached itself from them and started down the slope toward her. It was a man, his hands plunged deep into his pockets. She realized it was Johnny. She rose, starting toward him.

The wind played with the glossy waves of his blue-black hair and reddened his smooth skin — succeeding, it occurred to Jane, in making him look even more handsome. A dangerous handsomeness. She felt a loathing for him rise up inside her. Keeping her face expressionless, she walked toward him.

He took her in with a glance, then looked all around, as if checking for observers. Apparently satisfied, he returned his gaze to Jane and said, "So Ivy got herself killed?"

She gave him a look of scornful disbelief. "You know she did. Carla must have told you." An especially strong gust of wind rattled them both, and she shivered. "Why did we have to meet here?"

"Why not? It's open, healthy . . ."

"Safe for you."

He shrugged. "So what do you want? Why do you want to talk to me? If it's about Ivy getting killed, I don't know nothin' about it."

"Johnny, who was the man with the gun?"

He smiled slyly. "Ah, the man with the gun. What's it to you?"

"Would you rather tell the police?"

His smile was gone. "I told you what would happen to you if you called the police. Don't try it, Jane. I mean it."

She was overwhelmed by a wave of revulsion for him. "What are you going to do, hit me?" She laughed in disgust. "Make sure you do it in a place that doesn't show. Coward. Bully."

He gave his head an uncaring toss and wet his lips. "That what you came here to say to me? I guess we're done, then."

"No, we're not. Ivy told me you only came to the retreat to get away from that man. She said you and he had had some 'business dealings.' "

"Business dealings," he repeated with a little laugh, "I like that. That's right."

"What happened to him?"

His face underwent a chilling change, as if behind those beautiful eyes he was reliving something cold and ugly. "Let's just say we . . . came to an understanding."

Staring at him, Jane swallowed. Then she shivered, but not from the cold. Pushing a lock of hair back out of her face, she said, "Johnny, why were you interested in Ivy in the first place? You know, good-looking guy like you."

"Why do you think?"

"I honestly can't imagine. I doubt it was for her looks."

He looked at her, saying nothing.

Jane said, "Her personality?"

"Oh, did she have one? No, it was because of her job. She worked at *Skyline*, remember? I was using her."

"In what way?"

"To find out if the newspaper had any information on one of my, uh, 'dealings.' I'd heard a rumor they did. I'd found out which editor was working on the story, figured out who his secretary was — Ivy — and 'accidentally' met her at some party I knew she'd be at."

He laughed, remembering. "She was wild about me. She agreed to help me right away. She kept saying she was trying to help me find out what I wanted to know, but she never did. Now I think she was stringing me along, stalling so I wouldn't dump her."

Poor Ivy. . . . Jane nodded sadly. "I'm sure that was true."

"And that's it," he said simply. "End of story. I got nothin' more to tell you." He stood waiting, his wind-reddened face nestled into his upturned collar.

She couldn't bear to look at him another minute. She turned and started back toward Fifth Avenue.

★ ★ ★

Jane hadn't originally planned to go to the office between Christmas and New Year's — she never did — but as she alighted from the bus in Shady Hills and made her way toward her car, she realized that some time there might lift her spirits, help restore a sense of normalcy.

As she drove around Center Street, she noticed a sign in the window of Whipped Cream that said: NEW YEAR'S EVE LUNCH SPECIALS. She'd completely forgotten it was the last day of the year. Stanley was coming over. She would have to find out if Florence would be staying in, plan dinner, pick up what she needed. She wouldn't stay long at the office.

She drove past her agency's front door and turned right into the narrow alley that led to the parking lot behind the building. Pulling into a space, she glanced up at the back door of the office, in the top half of which was a window. The lights were on. She frowned in puzzlement.

Entering the office, she found Daniel at his desk, typing away on his computer. He looked up, startled. "What are you doing here?"

"I might ask you the same thing."

He shrugged. "Just thought I'd grab the

time to do some catching up. Ginny had to work today anyway."

She went up behind him and gave him an affectionate pat on the shoulder. "We're both nuts, I think. But thanks, Daniel."

Over his shoulder he gave her a sympathetic smile.

She said, "We'll make it . . . 'Work Lite' today, how's that? And I'll take you to lunch at Whipped Cream so we can see Ginny."

"Sounds great," he said, and glanced up at the wall clock above his monitor. It was nearly twelve-thirty. "Let me finish this letter and I'm ready."

She went into her office and smiled affectionately at the immense pile of work in the middle of her desk. She'd given up long ago trying to be organized. She was one of those people who got more done by staying messy. Early in their relationship, Daniel had tried valiantly several times to make sense of "The Heap," as he called it, but he only made things worse. She could never find anything. To others it looked like a heap, but to her it was comfortable and consistent, and it did have a loose sort of order to it. For instance, Daniel always placed her pink phone slips at the very center of the pile. There was one there now, and she frowned, surprised.

It said, "Please call Judy Monk, *Skyline*," and was followed by a New York City phone number.

"Daniel," she called, "who's this Judy Monk?"

He appeared in the doorway. "I meant to mention that to you. She called about twenty minutes ago. She said she works with Ivy. I could tell she didn't know about what happened. I didn't feel it was my place to tell her."

Jane sat down behind her desk and dialed the number.

"Judy Monk."

"Yes, hello, this is Jane Stuart, returning your call."

"Oh, yes, thanks so much for getting back to me. I'm not sure you can help me. I work for a newspaper called *Skyline* in New York. One of my co-workers hasn't shown up for work today, and she doesn't answer the phone at her apartment. I'm concerned because she and her boss have an important meeting today. It's not like her to just not show up. Her name is Ivy Benson."

"Yes, I know," Jane said. "How did you get my number?"

"It was in Ivy's Rolodex. It was the only

214

number that wasn't a business connection, if you know what I mean."

"Yes, I'm — I mean, I was her friend."

"Was? I . . . don't understand."

"Ms. Monk, I'm terribly sorry to tell you that Ivy is dead."

There was a sharp intake of breath. "Dead?"

"Yes. Were you and she close?"

"Well," Judy Monk said on an expulsion of breath, "I don't know that I'd say we were close, but we had a friendly relationship. I liked her. My cubicle is right next to hers. How did she die?"

"She . . . fell on some ice, hit her head. It happened last Thursday night. A terrible shock."

"Oh, my goodness gracious," Judy said in a low voice. "I can't believe it. Let me ask you — do you know who I should call about picking up Ivy's things? Her brother stopped by here on Friday, but I don't have his telephone number."

Jane sat very still. Ivy, like Jane, had been an only child. "What did her brother look like?"

"A heavy man, thinnish hair. Why? Don't you know him?"

"Uh — she had several brothers."

"I see. Well, he said he had her phone

215

number, but not her address, so I gave it to him." Judy was silent a moment. "Odd that he didn't tell me about what happened to Ivy. He must not have known yet."

"What did he want?"

"He said Ivy had sent him for something in her desk. I let him look, but he didn't seem to find it."

Jane's thoughts spun. She realized she didn't have Ivy's address, either. She would need it, though.

"So do you know?" Judy asked.

"Know what?"

"Who can come for Ivy's things."

Jane reflected. Ivy had had no family. Marlene was gone, and Ivy had been long divorced from Ira. "I'll be happy to come," she said. "There's really no one else — since I don't know where her brothers are."

"You don't?"

"No. Ivy and they were . . . estranged."

"I'm not surprised. Ivy once mentioned to me that she had no one — no family, I mean. Come to think of it, I do remember her mentioning a Jane. She said you were her best friend."

Jane sat very still, a shiver of sadness moving over her. Her eyes welled with tears. With her free hand she played with the edge of a memo in the heap. "Yes, I was."

"Then I'm very sorry for you, too," Judy said. "If you could come, that would be most helpful."

"Not a problem. Tomorrow is New Year's Day. Would it be all right if I came on Wednesday?"

"Absolutely. Anytime convenient for you — I'm here from nine to five. Eight-fifty Third Avenue, between Fifty-first and Fifty-second, west side of the street."

Jane hung up. Judy Monk was obviously a trusting soul. She'd immediately accepted an impostor as Ivy's brother. Who was he? What was he looking for? Why did he want Ivy's address? On Wednesday Jane would need to get it from Judy, too. It shouldn't be difficult.

Returning from lunch, Jane and Daniel found a message on the answering machine.

"Yes, Tamara Henley here. Jane, if you could please give me a call as soon as possible, that would be marvelous." And she left her number.

Daniel frowned down at the machine. "What does *she* want?"

"Darned if I know. Probably wants me to read her manuscript."

She went into her office and called Tamara back.

"How are you, Jane? What an awful thing up there at that wretched place. And your friend, no less. In all the confusion I never got a chance to tell you how sorry I am."

"Thank you, Tamara, I appreciate that. Was that why you were calling?"

"Oh, good heavens no," Tamara said with a laugh. "I'm supremely embarrassed, but I must ask you. Foss and I are having some people over tonight for New Year's, and it suddenly occurred to me that it would be wonderful if you and your policeman friend could come. Around eight. I do hope you don't already have plans."

"Uh . . . I'm not sure, to be honest with you."

"Oh," Tamara said, flustered. "Well, if you'll check and let me know . . . Do come. I've invited Vick Halleran and Jennifer Castaneda from the retreat, and they've accepted. I'm also going to invite Daniel, that adorable assistant of yours, and his girlfriend. As far as I'm concerned, these are the only people at the retreat who had

218

any class — except for you and your friend, of course."

"Thanks, Tamara." If she only knew the catty things Jennifer had said about her. "It's very kind of you to think of us. I'll get right back to you."

"Priceless," Tamara breathed, and rang off.

Jane called Stanley.

"Oh, I don't know, Jane," he whined. "I didn't like her much. Snob."

"Of course she's a snob. But think about it. This is a chance for us — for you, I mean" — oops! — "to chat with her, to find out if she saw or heard anything pertinent to Ivy's murder."

"We've already 'chatted' with her, Jane."

"Only perfunctorily. Come on, Stanley, we don't have any other plans, not really. Don't be such an old poop. I want to see her house," she blurted out.

He sighed. "All right. Tell her yes. If I'm not mistaken, she lives at the bottom of that new street off Magnolia Place."

"That's right. Those homes are *huge*. I want to see it. Come for me around a quarter to eight."

"Yes, ma'am."

"Please," she added. "And pick up a nice bottle of champagne on your way. Not too cheap."

She had no sooner hung up than Daniel appeared in her doorway. "Are you going?"

"Yup. I'm eager to see her place. Has Tamara called you yet?"

"Yes, I just hung up from her. I'm going to ask Ginny if she wants to go. We had planned to have a quiet evening . . ."

"What is it with you men? Of course Ginny will want to go."

Laughing to herself, she picked up the phone and called Tamara to accept.

Chapter Nineteen

Tamara and Foss Henley lived in the bottommost of a string of contemporary mansions clinging to a cliffside on a street not far from where Jane lived. In fact, Jane reflected as Stanley parked behind a long line of cars, only a little over a year ago this spot had been a public dumping ground . . . the place where Ivy's daughter Marlene had died. Jane herself had nearly lost her life there.

It was a mild night and they decided to leave their coats in the car. Stanley made small talk as they approached the house, an enormous multiwinged structure of glass and stucco. "At the station we call this street 'Nouveau Row,' " he said.

"You don't know that all these people are nouveau," Jane said, gazing up the winding road at the other mansions dotting the cliffside. "The houses are new, that's all."

"Oh, these people are nouveau, all right. At least compared to people like Puffy and Oren Chapin," he said, referring to one of Shady Hills' matriarchs and her husband. "Now, this Foss Henley, he does something having to do with real estate. A developer, I think. Next door is Mark Radner, who's a top executive at Nabisco in East Hanover. I'm not sure about the next house, but the one above is Gloria and Ian Ianelli, who — well, let's just say I wouldn't be surprised if they knew Johnny."

She looked at him, her eyes widening. "I *see*. Why didn't you ever tell me all this before?"

He shrugged uncomfortably. "There's a lot I don't tell you."

"For now," she said, shooting him an ominous sidelong glance, and he returned it with a look of mild alarm.

They were on the paving-stone path, approaching the front door, an immense slab of glass behind which they could see a two-story Christmas tree that reminded Jane of Ellyn's, and people in party dress milling around.

The bell was answered by Tamara herself, wearing a sleekly simple deep-cranberry dress and a magnificent necklace of diamonds set in either white gold or platinum. Her tawny gold hair was swept up becomingly from her aristocratic face.

"So glad you could make it," she said, kissing Jane, who formally introduced her to Stanley.

"Lovely to meet you under happier circumstances," Tamara said. "Now come in and make yourselves at home. We've got lots to eat and drink." She glided away.

"Does she ever," Jane said, eyeing a lavish hors d'oeuvres table and then spotting a busy bar at the back of the cavernous living room. Then Jane saw Daniel and Ginny standing not far away, chatting, drinks in hand.

"Yoo-hoo," Jane called softly. Ginny's face lit up, and she hurried over, Daniel in tow.

"Can you believe this?" Ginny said.

Jane shook her head in wonder. The left wall of the room consisted entirely of gargantuan blocks of rough stone. In the center of this wall was a fireplace, also enormous, with a raised hearth. To the right of the fireplace stood an odd, six-foot tangle of what appeared to be rusted wires in the approximate shape of the number six. A sculpture, Jane realized. "How odd . . ."

"My dad had a piece like that in his office," said Daniel, whose late father had owned one of the country's most successful magazines. Daniel had grown up in affluence and seemed never to be fazed by it. He was, in fact, quite wealthy himself since his father's death; yet he showed no signs of this literal change of fortune.

"My lucky number, six," came Tamara's voice behind Jane and Daniel, who turned to her.

"Oh?" Jane said.

"Mm. It's always been that way. I met Foss on the sixth of June. Our daughter was born on the sixth of December. It was on the sixth of August that our accountants told us we were officially millionaires. I could go on and on."

I'll bet you could, Jane thought. "Three sixes . . ." she said with a mischievous smirk. "The mark of the devil. Warner Books and Bantam Doubleday Dell were once at 666 Fifth Avenue."

"Of course they were," Daniel joined in, and they both laughed.

Tamara appeared to have heard none of this exchange. "Come," she said to Jane, "I want you to meet my husband."

Jane slid a glance at Daniel, who appeared not to care that Tamara hadn't included him. He winked at Jane and wandered away. Meanwhile, Tamara had fetched her husband and was leading him over, a man in a fawn cashmere jacket and black slacks. Around sixty, he was of medium height, balding, with a paunch. His features were coarse in comparison with Tamara's finely cut, aristocratic ones. As he took Jane's hand, his face bloomed into a handsome smile.

"Ah, our illustrious literary agent," he said. "Such a pleasure. Thank you for humoring my wife."

Tamara turned to him in feigned indignation. "Foss! Whatever do you mean?"

"Tell me honestly, Mrs. Stuart —"

"Please call me Jane."

"Jane. Is my wife the next Danielle Steel?"

"Maybe not yet," Jane said with good humor, "but she may very well be on her way." She laughed, and they all laughed with her.

"I never said I was the next Danielle Steel," Tamara pouted. "I said my books resembled hers." She gave him a dismissive flip of her hand. "What do you know anyway, wrapped up in your boring old buildings?"

He rolled his eyes good-naturedly. "Pleasure to have you with us," he said, gave them both a conspiratorial wink, and moved on.

Tamara positioned herself in front of Jane, as if the others were no longer there. "How are you doing, Jane?" she said with a sad little frown. "I mean, about your friend?"

"I'm doing all right, Tamara. Thank you for asking."

"Poor little thing," Tamara said, eyes unfocused, remembering. "She was so happy the last time I saw her."

"Where was that?" From the corner of her eye, Jane saw Stanley look away in exasperation.

Tamara caught it, too, and turned to him. "Is something wrong?"

Stanley laughed. "No, nothing, except that I wish Jane would realize she's a literary agent, not a police detective."

Jane feigned hurt surprise. "I've made *some* progress on this case, Stanley, you have to admit it. You know you want my help; you're just not allowed to say so. Besides, Ivy was very close to me. I've got a special stake in this."

"Of course you do," Tamara said.

Jane gave her a grateful smile. "Now, as I was saying, where was the last place you saw Ivy?"

"It was in the lounge," Tamara said. "Ivy was coming back inside with Jennifer. They'd gone out to have a cigarette. Ivy was laughing so hard, brushing the snow off her green sweater." Her face grew solemn and she turned to include Stanley in the conversation. "I'll tell you something I noticed, though. That despicable Larry Graham was watching Ivy and had an odd gleaming look in his eye, kind of . . . preoccupied. Then he left the room. What do you make of that?"

Stanley opened his mouth, but no words came out. Jane, too, was at a loss, but Jane was never at a loss for long. "It's so hard to say. Maybe he was attracted to her."

"Maybe. But of course Ivy was already seeing that Johnny character. Nasty doings," she cried, raising her index finger. Then she shrugged. "At any rate, my dear, you have my deepest sympathy. Now do relax and try to have a good time. There are some frightful people over there I must be nice to."

She walked off, leaving a heavy cloud of rose and violet in her wake.

"Let's mingle," Jane told Stanley, Daniel, and Ginny, and began drifting through the crowd. Near the bar she spotted Vick Halleran and Jennifer Castaneda, their heads close together, their expressions intense. She hurried over to them. "Good evening."

They both turned to her, huge smiles instantly appearing.

"How lovely to see you," Jane said, exchanging kisses with them both. Vick, wearing a blue blazer over a silk crew-neck T-shirt and gray slacks, looked as if he'd managed to gain at least ten pounds in the three days since Jane had last seen him. Jennifer, on the other hand, looked smashing in a gold lamé jumpsuit. "You both look fabulous."

"So do you," Jennifer squealed.

"You both remember Stanley Greenberg," Jane said, urging him forward.

For a moment they both stared at him, as if trying to place him. Then recognition dawned, and with it came puzzlement.

"Yes, of course," Vick said nervously. "How are you?"

"Fine, thank you," Stanley said stiffly.

"Don't worry," Jane said, "he's not here to interrogate you. He's . . . my date."

"Ah," Jennifer said, and giggled, looking Stanley up and down. Her gaze dropped to the empty glass in her hand. "Oops — empty. Excuse me."

Vick watched Jennifer walk away toward the bar, his expression uneasy. Jane remembered Carla saying he had looked "uncomfortable" when Jennifer entered the lounge the night of Ivy's murder. Why? Jane wondered. Could it have had something to do with Ivy? Did Vick know something he hadn't revealed? Jane yearned to bring it up but didn't dare do so with Stanley at her side. At any rate, Jennifer reappeared a moment later, holding a glass full of an amber drink. She seemed suddenly aware that Vick was still there, and her expression grew tense.

"I think I need a refill too," he said, and turned to Stanley and Jane. "See you both in a bit."

"Of course," Jane said, eyeing him curiously, and watched him walk, shoulders hunched, to the bar.

Jennifer, at ease again, focused on Jane. "Now. Let's talk about books, something we never got to do at the lodge."

Jane frowned in bafflement. "The entire retreat was about writing books."

"*My* books. You're an agent," Jennifer said, as if Jane didn't know. "What trends do you see? What should I be doing differently? There's always room for improvement."

"To be honest, Jennifer, I haven't read you."

Jennifer blinked hard. "You haven't read me? Nothing? Not even *Heat of the Night*?" This book, Jane knew, was her most recent hardcover, her biggest book yet.

"No," Jane said, wincing. "I'm sorry," she squeaked.

"No, no, don't be silly." Jennifer's gaze wandered. "Oh, I see someone I haven't said hello to. Will you excuse me?"

"Certainly," Jane said, and shot Stanley a look as the beautiful young woman slipped away through the crowd.

"Are *your* authors like that?" he asked.

"Eventually," she replied dryly and, taking his arm, propelled him through the crowd toward the food table.

They couldn't leave before midnight, of course, but once they had all shouted "Happy New Year!" and exchanged kisses and thrown black and white streamers across the room in every direction, Jane realized she was pooped.

"Let's go," she said softly to Stanley.

"Thank you," he said, raising his eyes heavenward.

"Oh, stop it. This wasn't so bad. We've met some interesting people, seen how the other half lives."

He shrugged. They said good night to Daniel and Ginny, then found Tamara, who was with her husband chatting with another couple, and told her they had to be going.

"We'll see you out," Tamara said, grabbing Foss and telling the other couple they would be back in a bit. When they reached the foyer, she turned to them. "Coats?"

"In the car," Jane said.

"Well, it's wonderful of you both to come," Tamara said. "We must get together again." She winked at Jane. "You're my kind of people."

Stanley said nothing, merely looked uncomfortable, and Jane, realizing she had to say something, blurted out, "Definitely. Well . . ." she said, kissing Tamara's cheek, and turned toward the door. As she did, she noticed a large sepia-toned photograph in an elaborate frame hanging on one of the foyer's stone walls.

"Pretty, isn't it?" Tamara said softly, coming up beside her. Jane was aware of Foss on her other side.

Jane studied the photograph. It was of a beautiful old neo-Gothic church with many pointed arches and a kind of interwoven tracery Jane had never seen before. "What church is that?"

Foss said, "It's St. Paul the Apostle Church in New York City. It was designed by a disciple of Cass Gilbert."

"The famous American architect," Tamara said.

"Yes, I know." Jane continued to study the picture.

"The photo itself is a work of art," Tamara said dramatically. "I simply had to have it. Foss and I paid a fortune for it at auction. We'll walk you out."

Outside, the air was refreshingly brisk. Jane breathed deeply, gazing up into a clear, starry sky. Then her gaze lowered and landed on a house across the street. She blinked. The structure could not have been more incongruous with the surrounding homes. It was a small, older home, quite shabby, and not much bigger than the house William Ives occupied with his granddaughter and great-granddaughter.

"The bane of our existence," Tamara said, glaring at it.

"It . . . needs some work," Jane said diplomatically.

"Oh, you don't have to worry about us," Tamara said. "You can be honest. It's a shack. It's in shockingly bad repair. You see, the people who live there are *renters*." She spoke the word as if she were saying *lepers*.

"I see," Stanley said, all seriousness.

"They don't do a thing to maintain the place. And ultimately," Tamara went on in a regretful tone, "the house's owner — a friend of ours, actually — will be blamed. Hardly fair."

She drew her gaze from the dilapidated house and returned it to Jane and Stanley. "Well, good night, my dears, and thank you again for coming. Jane, I'll call you about doing lunch."

Jane smiled, but behind her smile she was already composing a list of excuses.

Chapter Twenty

Jane spent New Year's Day at home with Nick. Florence had gone to visit her friend Noni. Jane had given Florence a list of the kittens' names and descriptions, reminding her that Noni had said she wanted one.

Stanley had promised to spend the day with his younger sister, Linda, who was divorced and lived with her twelve-year-old daughter, Ashley, at the north end of town.

Winky and the kittens, whose eyes still had not opened, were a constant source of entertainment. Nick, stationed on a chair he had carried into the laundry room, looked up from a spiral notebook in which he'd started to record which kittens nursed at what times.

"Why are you doing that?" Jane asked, amused.

"Just keeping track of things," he replied, his expression intense as he watched the tiny creatures get their nourishment.

She looked over his shoulder and smiled. He glanced up, sensing her presence, and in his look, at that moment, she saw so much of Kenneth in his face that her breath caught in her throat. She still missed him terribly, even though he had died more than three years ago. She probably always would. Yet somehow the pain had lost its sharp edge. She guessed that was due to time, and to Stanley.

"Why are you wearing that apron?" Nick asked.

"Because I'm making New Year's dinner, remember? Florence is coming back in time for it."

"What are you making?" he asked warily.

"All kinds of good stuff. Caesar salad, rack of lamb —"

"Blech. I hate those things. Can I have chicken fingers?"

"No, you may not have chicken fingers. You'll like what I'm making," she said, though she didn't necessarily believe that. "Besides, for dessert I bought a chocolate cream pie."

"Now, *that* I'll eat."

She turned to leave the room.

"Mom?"

"Mm?"

"Can we keep all the kittens? I'm afraid it will make Winky sad if we only let her keep one."

She gave him a kind smile. "I'm afraid we can't, honey. Two cats are enough for this household. And Winky knows we'll only give her babies to good homes."

His gaze dropped as he thought this over; then he nodded and returned to his recording. Jane headed back to the kitchen, from which came the tantalizing aroma of lamb roasting with garlic and rosemary.

At around eight o'clock that evening, Stanley called. He was home from Linda's. Would Jane like to come over for a drink? Jane had finished cleaning up after dinner, but felt funny leaving Nick.

"Don't you think twice about it, missus," said Florence, who had returned from Noni's earlier that day with a promise to take Crush. She gave Jane a mischievous wink. "In fact, if you need to be out for the night, that's okay, too."

Jane felt herself blush. "No, thank you, Florence — though I appreciate the offer."

That night, in Stanley's plant-filled apartment, they sipped brandy and danced slowly to his collection of Frank Sinatra LPs, and Jane pressed her cheek softly against Stanley's and closed her eyes.

"Happy New Year!" Daniel greeted her at the office the next morning.

"Same to you. Hope you and Ginny had

a nice day yesterday."

"Mm, a quiet day, the kind I like best."

"Did you enjoy Tamara's party Monday night?"

He smiled, wrinkled his straight nose a little. "Not very much, to be honest. I find her hard to take."

"I know what you mean."

"He seems very down to earth, though. The husband, I mean. What kind of name is Foss, do you know?"

"I believe it's short for Forrest."

He looked down thoughtfully at his keyboard, then resumed entering information into the database they used to record details of the book deals they made for their clients.

Later that morning, Jane took the Lakeland bus into New York and cabbed to Fifty-second and Third. On the seventeenth floor, a plump, prim-looking woman emerged into the reception area and introduced herself as Judy Monk.

"Let me say again how sorry I am about poor Ivy," she said in a low, solemn voice, her eyes full of kindness. "I'll show you where her office is — was." She led Jane back through a nondescript maze of cubicles and stopped at the entrance to one of them. "This is it."

She allowed Jane to go in first. A desk without much on it stood against the cubicle's back wall, so that Ivy would have had her back to the entrance when she was working. Above the desk was a bulletin board on which had been pinned what appeared to be several publication schedules. Then Jane noticed, at the extreme lower right corner, a photograph of Ivy and Jane herself, taken when they were freshman roommates at the University of Detroit twenty-one years earlier. "Oh, my goodness," Jane murmured, moving closer to the photo. The two young women — Ivy, chubby, with brown curly hair; Jane, reed thin, with straight reddish-brown hair — were smiling intently into the camera, their arms tightly around each other's waist.

Judy came up beside Jane. "My word. It's the two of you, isn't it? You *do* go way back."

"Yes, we do," Jane said sadly.

"Well." Judy surveyed the desk as if unsure where to direct her gaze. "I'm sure she was very lucky to have a good friend like you."

Jane met Judy Monk's gaze directly. "Thank you, but in all honesty, I'm not sure I was always a very good friend to her."

Judy's jaw dropped a little, and she gave a serious, bewildered nod. She gestured toward the desk. "I suppose I could have shipped her things to you, now that I think of it. There's not much here."

Jane regarded the desk, on which sat a keyboard and monitor, an uncluttered blotter, a telephone, a Rolodex, and a framed photograph of Ivy's late daughter, Marlene.

"That was her daughter," Judy said. "I know she passed away, but I don't know how." She kept her gaze on Jane, as if waiting for an answer.

"It was . . . an accident," Jane said, feeling for some reason that the truth was probably more than Ivy would have wanted Judy to know.

"How very sad," Judy said. "You know, I liked Ivy but never got to know her very well, even though she worked here for a good six months. She seemed that kind of person. Private. One thing we all knew, though. She had ambition." There was admiration in the statement.

"Really?" Jane said, turning to her. "Why do you say that?"

"She made no secret of the fact that she believed she was better suited to the job of reporter, in spite of the fact that she'd been hired as a secretary. She told me once that she hated being a secretary and that a job like that was unworthy of her. She said that back in Detroit she held a much higher position."

Jane's heart went out to her poor dead friend, who'd needed to impress strangers with lies. In Detroit, Ivy had been a secretary at an insurance agency. "Yes, I believe she did."

Judy looked disappointed that this was all she was apparently going to get out of Jane. "I can believe it. She told me several times that she intended to be a reporter for this paper. In fact, there was one particular story she was after. Quite often she ran out of the office telling me she was following up on 'that story.' "

"Interesting. Did she tell you what the story was?"

"Oh, no. She wouldn't tell anyone. But she did say that when she was finished getting it, *Skyline* would promote her to reporter."

"Do you think that was true?"

"To tell you the truth," Judy replied, "I don't think she would have made it that far."

Jane frowned. "What do you mean?"

"Mr. Feingold was frustrated with her.

He hired her to be his secretary, but she hated the work and was — I shouldn't say this — rather poor at it. I suppose I can say this now . . . I believe Ivy was about to get fired."

"I see," Jane said, and sat down in Ivy's chair.

"I'll leave you to it. I brought you a box." Judy indicated a smallish cardboard carton on the floor to the right of the desk and started out of the cubicle.

Jane thanked her and set to work. Judy was right; there wasn't much here. Clearly Ivy had kept her personal life out of the office, except for the two photographs. Otherwise, Jane found only some makeup, an extra pair of shoes in the bottom left-hand drawer, and a rose-colored pullover sweater neatly folded in the drawer above it. There were no files in Ivy's desk, Jane noticed. The only papers were company-wide memos, takeout menus from local restaurants, photocopies of some not-very-important letters Ivy had typed for her boss, Andrew Feingold. Puzzled, Jane rose and went in search of Judy. She found her in the next cubicle, typing very fast. She gave a little jump, putting her hand to her breast, and turned. "Done already?"

"Not quite. A couple of questions, if you don't mind."

"Not at all," Judy said graciously.

"There aren't any files in Ivy's desk, and there's no file cabinet either. Do you find that odd?"

Judy drew her thick brows together. "I do find that odd. Mr. Feingold has asked me to gather up Ivy's files and deal with them, but I haven't had a chance to do it yet." She shook her head in bafflement. "I suppose she carried her files with her. Now that I think about it, she did carry a brief-case every day. It's the only explanation. As I told you, she was working on something she was keeping a secret, so it would make sense that she wouldn't leave the files lying around."

"What about her computer? Would there be files there?"

Judy gave Jane a strange look, as if wondering why Jane would want to know that. "Actually, no," she said slowly. "Everything is stored on the main server, nothing locally. These computers don't even have hard drives of their own."

"I see. Thanks."

With a chill at the memory of the man who had posed as Ivy's brother, Jane remembered she would have to check Ivy's apartment. Now that she thought about it, she was, as far as she knew, the only person Ivy had in the world who could dispose of her belongings at home, just as she was the only person who could take away Ivy's personal items here in the office.

Jane returned to Ivy's cubicle and finished up. The last items she placed in the box were Ivy's two photos. Jane gazed wistfully at the one of both of them, then placed it atop the rest of Ivy's things. As she rose from the chair, something on Ivy's blotter caught her eye. Ivy had been a doodler. There were diamond patterns, sketches of girls with long, pretty hair, and a recurrent image of two palm trees, trunks crossed, six coconuts lined up at the base of their trunks. Yes, Jane remembered, this would have been just like Ivy — Ivy who never dressed warmly enough, Ivy who daydreamed about her happier, carefree someday life in the tropics. Ivy who had yearned for a better life, a better job, a good man.

Taking a deep breath, Jane picked up the box and went to tell Judy she was finished. She found Judy on the telephone, apparently with her boss. She gestured to Jane that she would be a moment. Hanging up, she said, "Thank you so much for doing this. Again, I'm so sorry about Ivy." She smiled kindly. "I'm sure you *were* a good friend to her."

"Thank you." Jane set down the box on the floor. "Judy, I wonder if you could give me Ivy's address." Ivy had never given it to Jane, nor had Jane found it among Ivy's things.

"Her address?" Judy frowned. "I don't understand. Wouldn't you have it? If you and she . . ." Now she eyed Jane with some alarm, as if wondering if she'd made a mistake giving this woman access to Ivy's cubicle.

Jane gave a little laugh. "I guess it does seem like an odd request. You see, Ivy and I had a falling-out. We didn't speak for over a year. Then she moved to New York and we patched things up, but that was only a few weeks ago. I hadn't been to her apartment yet, and I never got around to getting her address."

Judy lowered her gaze, considering. "Well," she said, looking up, "I suppose I could get it from Mr. Feingold's secretary."

"I'd be so grateful. I've got to take care of her things."

"Of course. One moment."

Judy went down the passage and disappeared into a cubicle at the end. She reemerged a moment later holding a slip of paper. "Here you are," she said, and glancing down at the writing on the paper before handing it to Jane, stopped and frowned. "That's odd."

"What?"

"This address. It couldn't be right."

Jane craned her neck to see it. "Why not?"

Judy showed it to her. It was an address on West 38th Street, with an apartment number. Jane looked at her, not understanding.

"This is Hell's Kitchen," Judy said.

"Right . . ." Jane still didn't understand.

Judy met her gaze. "But Ivy lived in Sutton Place."

Jane blinked. "Come again?"

"It's true," Judy said solemnly. "I was kind of shocked, too, when she told me. But she said she inherited an apartment there from her aunt. You don't think it's true?"

Gently, Jane took the slip of paper from Judy's hand. "I'll check out *this* address first," she said, avoiding the question.

Now Judy looked thoroughly stumped. "All right," she said softly. Her hand was limp when Jane shook it before picking up the box and saying good-bye.

Chapter Twenty-one

Jane paid the cab driver and got out, then lifted out the box of Ivy's belongings. As the cab pulled away, she turned and looked up at the grimy five-story brownstone a few doors west of Eighth Avenue. Sutton Place it most definitely was not.

Carrying the box, she climbed the seven steps into the vestibule and consulted the address Judy Monk had given her. Apartment 5-C. On the wall to the right was a list of names next to buzzers. Beside 5-C was written JORDAN. Frowning in puzzlement, Jane pressed the buzzer. There was no answer. On an impulse she tried the door into the building, but it was locked tight. She rang the buzzer again. Nothing.

The door from the street opened, and a woman who appeared to be in her late sixties and carried a sack of groceries trudged in. She was quite heavy, her flesh straining against the pink sweater and skirt she wore under a man's oversized tan parka, its hood lined with ratty fake fur. Seeing Jane, she stopped and looked her up and down, her expression wary. "Who you lookin' for?"

"Ivy Benson," Jane replied.

"Not home. Ain't been home since before Christmas."

"You know her, then?" Jane said, brightening a little.

The woman let out a single high-pitched cackle. "Oughta know her. Rents a room from me." Jane noticed that the woman had no teeth, her mouth puckering in around her gums.

"Then you're the — superintendent here?" Jane asked doubtfully.

"No," the woman cried impatiently. "I just told you, she rents a room from me. In my apartment."

Then Ivy hadn't even had a place of her own. "I see."

"And who are you?"

"My name is Jane Stuart. I'm an old friend of Ivy's."

"So?"

"I'm here because — well, I'm afraid I have some bad news about Ivy. She's dead."

"Well, if she's dead," the woman replied without missing a beat, as if she'd just been told the toilet was leaking, "why are you looking for her?"

Jane forced a little smile. What a perfectly horrid woman. "You're right, of course. I'm here because Ivy had no family. I was pretty much the only person she had. I came to get her things."

"Damn straight you better take her things," the woman said, starting up the staircase that hugged the left wall of the corridor. " 'Cause now I gotta rent that room again. Don't need all o' her junk in there."

Jane, still clutching the box, started up the stairs after her. The stairway smelled of unwashed bodies and disinfectant but most of all of garlic, a stench of garlic so strong that it seemed to come from the very walls, like sweat through the pores of skin.

Abruptly the woman stopped and looked down at Jane with a scowl. "Hey, how do I know you're really who you say you are?"

"I beg your pardon?" Jane said, confused.

"How do I know this isn't some trick to get into my apartment, to take my stuff?"

Oh, for pity's sake. "Look, Mrs. —"

"Jordan. It says it on the buzzer."

"Mrs. Jordan —"

"*Miss* Jordan."

"I'm sorry. Miss Jordan. If you need

some kind of proof, I'm sure I could get it for you." Then Jane remembered the photo from Ivy's cubicle. "Wait, I do have something." She rummaged in the box and found the photo of herself with Ivy when they were freshmen. She held it out for Miss Jordan to see.

The older woman looked at the photo for a moment, then shifted her gaze to Jane. "Decided to go redhead in your old age, I see," she said, and chuckled at her own wit as she resumed her trudge up the stairs.

"Auburn," Jane said.

"What?" Miss Jordan squawked.

"My hair is auburn, not red."

Miss Jordan ignored her.

Jane was out of breath and her legs felt rubbery and weak by the time they reached the fifth floor and Miss Jordan put down her grocery bag to take out her key and open the door of apartment 5-C.

"Well, come on," Miss Jordan said impatiently, and Jane followed her inside. Miss Jordan crossed a small, shabbily furnished living room and entered a tiny kitchen, where she began putting away her groceries.

Jane said, "How long has Ivy been your, um, roommate?"

Miss Jordan slammed down a frozen half-gallon of Breyer's chocolate-chip ice cream onto the counter. "I *told* you, she rented a room from me. This is *my* apartment." She pointed down a short hallway leading off the living room to Jane's right. "Her room is the one on the left. I'd appreciate it if you'd hurry up with whatever you need to do. I've got plans tonight."

"Sure, no problem," Jane said, hating this woman, and carrying the box she still held down the hallway, pushed open the door on the left. She gasped.

The room had been ransacked. The mattress of the single bed had been stripped of sheets and bedding and leaned against the wall. The box spring shot out at almost a right angle to the bed itself. The six drawers of a dresser on the other side of the room had all been yanked out, their contents rifled and dumped. A pale green oval chenille area rug had been tossed on top of a grimy white vinyl clothes hamper.

Miss Jordan's footsteps sounded in the hallway. "You know, I was just thinkin', there ain't no way you're gonna get all her stuff —" She appeared in the doorway and froze, shooting her gaze around the room. "What the hell d'you do in here?"

"It wasn't me and you know it," Jane

said. "When was the last time you were in this room?"

Miss Jordan looked at Jane aghast. "What, you think *I* did this?"

"No," Jane said wearily. "I'm trying to figure out when this happened."

"I don't ever come in here. Why would I? It's Ivy's room, her privacy."

"Well, someone came in here, between the morning of Saturday, the twenty-second — that's the day Ivy came out to visit me in New Jersey — and now. No one broke into this apartment, apparently —"

Miss Jordan nodded in agreement.

"— which means it was someone with a key, or you let someone in."

"I didn't let nobody in," Miss Jordan cried defensively, gums flapping.

"Who else has a key to the apartment besides you and Ivy?"

"Just the super."

"You'd better call him."

"Damn straight I better." Miss Jordan stomped back down the hall to the kitchen. From the doorway of Ivy's room Jane watched her dial the phone.

"Yeah, Rafael," Miss Jordan barked into the receiver, "it's Marie. Get up here. Now."

Jane glanced back into Ivy's room. There

was no point in looking around. If there had been anything there to find, Johnny — for who else could it have been? — had no doubt found it. Ivy's briefcase, for instance.

Still carrying the box of Ivy's belongings from *Skyline,* Jane returned to the living room and waited awkwardly in the center of the room while Miss Jordan put away more groceries.

"You can sit," Miss Jordan said, more like an order than an offer.

Behind Jane was a sofa covered with a fluffy tan throw. She set down the box and approached the sofa.

"Hold it," Miss Jordan barked from the kitchen. "What do you think you're doin'?"

This woman really was too much. "I beg your pardon?"

"Flopsie. Mopsie. Cottontail. Vamoose!"

The fluffy tan throw stirred, and Jane realized now that it was, in fact, three Persian cats sleeping in a tight clump. At Miss Jordan's command they stood, stretched, and bounded off the sofa, leaving a matted thatch of shedded fur in their place.

Jane had second thoughts about the sofa and headed for a nice clean vinyl chair, when there was a knock on the door. Miss Jordan opened it to reveal a slight middle-aged man with thinning black hair and a full mustache. He wore jeans and a black hooded sweatshirt.

"What is it?" He spoke with a faint Hispanic accent.

"You let anybody into my apartment since —" Miss Jordan turned to Jane inquiringly.

Jane said, "Since the morning of the twenty-second."

He stared hard at Jane, as if she'd just materialized. Then his gaze darted back to Miss Jordan, fear in his eyes. "Uh . . ." he said, as if trying to guess the right answer.

"Yes or no!" Miss Jordan shrieked, stomping her foot.

He jumped. "Um, yes!" He smiled, almost triumphantly, as if now he would win the prize. "The roach man!"

Miss Jordan scowled. "The roach man?"

"*Sí*. It was . . ." His gaze wandered. "Last Friday. You were not home."

"Just one problem, bozo," Miss Jordan said. "I don't got no roaches." Before he could respond, she took him by the wrist like a little boy, snapped, "Come," and led him down the hallway to Ivy's room. "Take a look at what you did."

He peered into the room. "*Dios mio!* Who did this?"

"Your roach man, that's who!" Miss Jordan moved close to Rafael, right in his face. "Why'd you let a stranger into my apartment without asking for no ID? What kind of super are you? I'm gonna call the police."

"Wait," Jane said, and they both turned to look at her. "Rafael, tell me, please, what did the man look like?"

"What did he look like?" He waved his hands frantically. "I don't know, like a man," he cried, his voice breaking.

Jane said, "Tall, short, fat, thin, blond hair, brown hair . . . ?"

"What's the difference?" Miss Jordan demanded.

"Because I need to find out who searched Ivy's room," Jane said, as if speaking to a cretin.

Miss Jordan looked as if she were about to clobber Jane. Her shoulders slowly rose. Jane wouldn't have been surprised to see steam shoot from her ears. "You're crazy, you know that?" she said in an ominously low voice. "I knew I shouldn't'a let you into my apartment." She poked her finger hard into Jane's chest. "Get the hell outta here."

"No, wait, please," Jane said, turning to Rafael. "This man. Was he young, dark-haired, good-looking?"

Rafael slid a scared look at Miss Jordan, afraid to speak, but finally he dared to shake his head. "No," he replied in a low voice. "No, that was not him. This man, he was balding, heavy."

Jane nodded, remembering how Judy Monk had described Ivy's "brother."

"I said *get out*," Miss Jordan screamed. "Get out! Crazy rich broads playing police," she muttered, and marched back to the phone, where quite distinctly Jane could see her dialing 911.

Jane looked back at Rafael. He shook his head and gave a helpless shrug of apology. Shaking her head, Jane picked up the box of Ivy's belongings, walked out of the apartment, and headed down the garlic-scented stairs.

"Miss?"

Jane turned. Rafael stood at the landing.

"Was Miss Ivy upset about her room?" He smiled sweetly. "She's a nice lady."

She went back up the stairs to the landing. "I'm sorry to tell you this," she said gently, "but Ivy . . . Ivy died."

His eyes grew wide. "Died? How?"

"She was at a retreat with me in New Jersey. Someone — she was murdered."

He slapped his hand over his mouth, as

if he himself had uttered the word. Jane gave a sad little nod.

Miss Jordan appeared in the doorway of her apartment. "You want to get arrested, lady?" she said in a vicious, piercing voice, " 'cause if you do, stick around. The cops are on their way."

They ignored her.

"Very nice lady," Rafael said, looking down. "She told me her story — about her daughter dying, about her marriage that didn't work. Not a happy life. But now . . . now things were better for her. A good job. It was taking her places, she said. And a new man who loved her." Jane made no response to this. "A man," Rafael continued, "who wanted to marry her."

Pity for her old friend pierced Jane's heart. "Did you meet him?" she asked.

"No, but Miss Ivy told me about him. He knows what happened to her?"

"Yes, he knows."

"He must have been very upset. Heart-broken."

Jane touched his hand resting on the banister, said good-bye, and shot Miss Jordan a cold look before starting down the stairs.

Rafael called after her, "Oh, there is someone else who should know about this."

She turned, waited.

"Her very best friend. They go way back, Miss Ivy said, all the way to college. Jane, her name is. Yes — Jane, that's it."

She stood very still. "Ivy told you about her?"

"*Sí*. The only person she had left in the world, she said — besides her boyfriend, of course. Miss Ivy said this friend Jane was always there for her, a true friend." His eyes narrowed, a thought occurring to him. "But you must know her, if you are also Miss Ivy's friend."

"Yes," she said softly, "I know her." Very slowly, she turned and started down the stairs.

"Miss?" Rafael called, and she turned again. He looked puzzled. "Who are *you?*"

She opened her mouth to speak, hesitated, closed it, and shook her head in quick apology. Turning again, she hurried down the stairs, the box of Ivy's belongings in her arms.

Outside, walking toward Eighth Avenue, she found she was crying. As she reached the avenue, a police cruiser passed her, turning onto 38th Street. She turned and watched it stop in front of Ivy's building.

Chapter Twenty-two

She walked, preoccupied, the box in her arms, up Eighth Avenue toward the Port Authority Bus Terminal.

Ivy hadn't changed at all. Still as competitive and insecure as ever, she had lied to Jane about her apartment and the kind of job she had. At *Skyline*, she had lied to Judy Monk, saying she lived at Sutton Place. Jane laughed out loud. She had to hand it to Ivy; she must have figured if she was going to lie, she might as well go all the way. Ivy had even felt compelled to lie to the slovenly Miss Jordan, who had referred to Jane and Ivy as "rich broads," and to Rafael, the superintendent, who believed Johnny wanted to marry Ivy.

Ivy's dreams, all lies.

Like her and Jane's friendship?

"You okay, ma'am?"

Startled, she looked up. A young police officer had approached her, his expression solicitous.

"Yes, I'm fine," she said. "Why?"

"I saw you crying . . . lugging that box and all."

"I'm fine," she repeated, "but thank you." She gave him a grateful smile, and he gave her a curt nod back. Then she crossed 40th Street and entered the bus terminal.

She checked her watch and realized she'd just missed the 3:00 P.M. Lakeland bus to Shady Hills. She decided a cup of coffee would taste very good right now, and went into a sandwich shop, settling at a small table with a large cappuccino and a chocolate almond biscotti.

As she sipped, the rush of commuters outside the café blurred and Ivy's ransacked room came into sharp focus.

Johnny had done that, of course. Not himself — he was too smart for that. The day after he killed Ivy, he hired some thug to pose as Ivy's brother to get her address out of Judy Monk, then as "the roach man," to do Johnny's ransacking for him. Obviously Johnny had decided that whatever he had told Ivy in confidence about his shady dealings was no longer safe. It made perfect sense: If he and Ivy had broken up because of Johnny's indiscretions with Carla Santino, Ivy would no longer feel any obligation to keep Johnny's secrets.

And so he had murdered her.

Then he had sent his man to search Ivy's

room for any incriminating notes, papers, files.

Jane frowned. One thing didn't make sense, though. Rafael had said he'd never met Johnny. In that case, Miss Jordan probably never had, either. Ivy wouldn't have wanted Johnny to see how she lived — her reason not to have given him her address.

Then if neither Rafael nor Miss Jordan knew Johnny, why did he feel a need to send someone else to search Ivy's room?

Jane shrugged. Perhaps the reason had nothing to do with whether Rafael and Miss Jordan knew Johnny. Perhaps Johnny had simply been unable to do it himself because of another commitment; perhaps he was somewhere too far away to get to the room as fast as he would have wanted to, and so he sent someone else. Perhaps it was simply that Johnny didn't want to run the risk of being identified later.

Had the searcher found what he was looking for? Jane wondered. If yes, then Johnny's job was done; he was safe; his secrets had died with Ivy. If no — the likelier scenario, for even Ivy would have been smart enough not to leave such information in such an insecure place — then he would keep looking, for Ivy must have made notes, written something about her story, somewhere. But where had she kept them?

Jane sat up sharply. But of course. *With her.* In her purse. *In her luggage.*

She frowned. What had happened to Ivy's handbag? To the big suitcase she'd brought with her from New York? Jane whipped out her cell phone and called Stanley. Buzzi at the desk said he was out, so she called his cell.

"And how is your new year so far?" he asked jovially.

"Fine."

"You don't sound very convincing."

After his demands that she stop playing detective, she was hesitant to ask him even one question about Ivy's case. But the worst that could happen was that he would say no. She hoped he still remembered what a good time they'd had at his apartment Tuesday night. Then, taking no chances, she decided to remind him. "You're a very good dancer, do you know that?"

"What?"

"I loved dancing to your Sinatra albums. Can we do that again soon?"

"Of course," he said, his voice relaxing. "But that's not why you called, is it?"

"Well, no, not exactly. Stanley, what happened to Ivy's purse and suitcase?"

"Her what?"

"Her things. The stuff she had with her at the retreat."

"Oh. Why?" he asked suspiciously.

Where to begin? She'd done so much without him to reach this point. "Stanley," she said, mustering her courage, "I have good reason to believe Ivy was murdered because of a story she was pursuing for the newspaper she worked for, *Skyline*."

"I'm listening."

"Last Friday — the day we found Ivy's body — someone got into Ivy's apartment pretending to be the exterminator and trashed it. I think whoever it was was looking for Ivy's notes, files, whatever she had written down about this story."

"And did this person find these notes et cetera?" he asked, sounding interested.

"We have no way of knowing. There's a chance he didn't. In which case, there's only one place those notes could be. In her handbag, in her suitcase — among the things she carried with her."

"So you're saying that if we go through Ivy's things and find out what story she was after, we'll know who killed her."

"Right. So." Energized, she sat up and

shook back her hair. "Where are her bag and suitcase?"

"Here at the station, of course."

"And can we have a look through them?"

"Sure, but it won't do us any good. We've already looked. Nothing in there but clothes, makeup, toiletries, and so on. Oh, I almost forgot, three issues of *The National Enquirer.* Jane," he said, a note of impatience coming into his voice, "do you really believe we didn't think of that?"

"Well . . . I didn't know if you knew about her job at the newspaper."

"Of course we did. Jane, when someone is killed — when we're conducting a murder investigation — we make it our business to find out all we can about the victim. Because it's true that, as you point out, clues from the victim's life almost always point to the identity of the killer."

She slumped back into her seat, toying with her coffee stirrer. "I see."

"Listen, if you want to look, come look."

"I don't see the point," she said lifelessly.

"But you can if you want. I certainly won't stop you."

She said, "Why are you being so cooperative? I thought you wanted me to stop playing detective?"

"I do. But it's no skin off my nose to

show you something like a suitcase and a pocketbook. Besides, these things will probably go to you eventually anyway. As far as we've been able to tell, Ivy had nobody. No relatives and few friends. You were the best friend she had."

That deep despair swept over her again and she saw Rafael's serious face before her, the big mustache moving as he said, *Miss Ivy said this friend Jane was always there for her, a true friend.*

"Are you there?"

"Yes. Sorry."

"You want to look, then?"

"No . . . On second thought, yes. I'll come by in the morning."

"Jane, are you all right? You sound odd. Sad or something."

"Sad or something?" she said, faintly amused. Really, were all men like Stanley? He really was a dear, but sometimes he could be so utterly clueless. "My best friend is gone, Stanley. Yes, I'm sad."

"Right," he said, abashed. "I'm sorry, Jane."

"It's all right," she said softly. "See you tomorrow."

Snapping her cell phone shut, she put on her coat. Then, with a deep sigh, she grabbed the box and headed through the crowd toward the escalator and Platform 405.

She passed the newsstand, which featured racks of books among the magazines. She spotted a paperback edition of Jennifer Castaneda's second-to-latest novel, *Mojito.*

She stopped and took down a copy. The cover depicted a beautiful golden-skinned Latina woman peering seductively out from under a huge straw hat in vivid circular stripes of fuchsia, canary, and lime. The hat reminded Jane of hats and bags she had seen at the straw markets in Antigua on her vacation the month before. In the woman's hand was a tall, wet highball glass of pale green liquid full of bubbles and ice cubes, a mint sprig on top — presumably the drink called the Mojito.

Then Jane realized that the woman under the hat was Jennifer Castaneda herself. Jane flipped the book over and gazed down at Jennifer's author photo, in which she was gazing out from under a much smaller hat. In all other respects the photograph was strikingly similar to the cover illustration.

An ambitious woman. Poor Vick Halleran. Had he had any idea of what he was getting himself into when he fell in love with Jennifer Castaneda?

Shaking her head, Jane replaced the book on the rack. She thought about Vick again, and realized all at once that while she was in New York, she really ought to see him. She moved to the edge of the crowd, set the box against the wall, found Vick's home number in her address book, and dialed it on her cell phone. It rang quite a few times, and she had almost decided to hang up when he answered.

"Hello, Jane. This is a pleasant surprise," he said, though he sounded puzzled and perhaps a bit uncomfortable to hear from her.

"Vick, I'm here in the city and wondered if I could take you to lunch. You busy?"

"Not anymore. I've just finished teaching my writing workshop at The New School — I had my home calls forwarded to my cell phone."

"Then you can do it?"

"I'd love to."

They arranged to meet at the school and go to lunch from there. Jane took a taxi to Twelfth and Sixth. Vick was waiting for her on the corner, a big smile on his round face.

"What a treat," he said, taking the box, which he insisted on carrying for her. "I can't remember when I've seen you so

266

many times in such a short period."

He led the way to a diner two blocks from the school and they took a booth. "So how are you, Vick?" she asked. "I'm sorry the retreat ended the way it did."

"It's certainly not your fault. What a horrible thing. That poor woman. Have the police got any leads?"

"No."

He lowered his gaze to his placemat, which bore a map of Greece. "The retreat wasn't going well for me anyway, Jane. I might as well tell you this now. Jennifer and I are getting a divorce."

"Oh, Vick," she said, putting her hand on his. "I'm so sorry."

He gave his head an uncaring little toss, though he still wouldn't look at her. "Last night Jennifer finally confessed she's still having an affair with her agent, Henry Silver. She's moving in with him." Finally he met her gaze. "I suppose it was pretty clear at the retreat that things weren't exactly right between Jennifer and me."

"Yes, I have to admit it was. I'm terribly sorry."

"Thanks, Jane, I appreciate that."

"Vick," she said, shifting in her seat. "There was something I wanted to talk to you about at Tamara's party Monday night, but I never got the chance."

"Oh?"

"Last Thursday night — the night before Ivy was found murdered — when Ivy and Jennifer came back into the lounge after they had their cigarettes, why did you look so uncomfortable?"

He blinked, brows lowered. "You weren't there, were you?"

"No."

"Then how do you know about it?"

"Carla told me."

He eyed her warily. He was quiet for a long moment, his face deeply troubled, his gaze fixed on the window beside their booth. The waiter arrived, and they ordered sandwiches.

Jane waited. Vick met her gaze, watched her for a brief moment, and seemed to make a decision. "It was because of something that had just happened," he said.

"Yes?" she prompted.

"In our room, before we went down to the lounge, Jennifer and I had a hideous fight. I accused her of continuing her affair with Henry. I said I would leave her if she didn't end it. She told me she was planning to leave me anyway; she just hadn't wanted to leave before her book was done."

He shook his head in wonder. "That's what she's like. A cold, calculating, ambitious monster. I've never met anyone like her. I loved her once, you know. I think I still do. But I never imagined that she was this kind of person."

Jane nodded sympathetically.

"There's more," he said. "Jennifer left our room, and I went downstairs a short time afterward. I went to the lounge and found her there. It was extremely uncomfortable for us both. After a short time, Jennifer announced she was going outside to have a cigarette. I'm positive she did this just to get away from me."

Jane said, "And Ivy went with her."

"That's right. As Jennifer walked out of the lounge, she tossed me a look" — his hands clenched — "this smug, self-satisfied expression that made my blood boil. It was like she was saying, 'I win.' I don't know. All I do know is that at that moment I decided to confront her again. I left the lounge and went outside. I saw Jennifer and Ivy standing together in the parking lot, a good distance away. They were smoking. As I made my way toward them, they separated. Ivy walked to the edge of the path that led to the pond and started down it . . ."

At this, Jane sat up straighter, listening intently.

". . . and I saw my chance to have it out with Jennifer. I hurried up to her. It was dim; the parking lot lights aren't very bright. I was furious as I approached her, got angrier and angrier the closer I got. I was so mad I thought I'd — I'd have a heart attack or something. Anyway, I walked right up to her and said, 'Listen, you ice bitch. If you leave me I'll sue you for everything you're worth. I'll ruin your career.' Then I grabbed her shoulder and spun her around — to discover, to my horror, that it wasn't Jennifer but Ivy. She was wearing Jennifer's white fisherman's knit sweater. Jennifer must have lent it to her."

"What did Ivy do?"

"She just stared at me. I was mortified, of course. I apologized to her, asked her to please forget it, and hurried back to the lodge.

"*That's* why I looked so uncomfortable when Jennifer and Ivy came back into the lounge. I was wondering if Ivy had told Jennifer what I said to her. I can't see how she wouldn't have."

"No," Jane agreed, "neither can I."

Their lunch arrived and they began to

eat, but neither of them was particularly hungry. They made awkward small talk about the publishing business, about the course Vick was teaching.

After lunch, outside on the sidewalk, she gave him a kiss and a tight hug and told him again how sorry she was and not to be a stranger. Then she watched him walk away, a sad, middle-aged man with lowered head and slumped shoulders.

Chapter Twenty-three

It was dark as Jane stared out the bus window at the buildings of Weehawken, thinking about what Vick had told her. Was that really all there was to it? Perhaps he was telling the truth as far as it went; perhaps he really had mistaken Ivy for Jennifer. But had he only spoken to her?

What if it had actually been Ivy who went down the path, and Vick followed her, thinking he was following Jennifer? What if Vick, in his fury toward Jennifer, had grabbed Ivy, mistaking her for his wife, and killed her?

Vick had always struck Jane as the sweetest, most gentle of men, but it was common knowledge that very often when this kind of person blew, he blew big-time.

But why would Vick have been carrying the ice pick?

Moreover, why would *Jennifer* have left Ivy and started down the path? What was she doing there? Back at her office, Jane decided simply to ask her. She finally tracked her down at Henry Silver's office.

"Jane," Jennifer said, as if speaking to a

272

child, "you can't call me here."

"Why not?"

"Because I'm — I'm busy. I'm in a meeting. What is it you want?"

"I just want to ask you a question." When Jennifer made no response, Jane went on, "Last Thursday night, when you and Ivy went outside to smoke your cigarettes, why did you leave Ivy and go down the path that leads to the pond?"

"How do you know I did that?"

Jane hesitated, then said, "Vick told me. He also told me about his mistaking Ivy for you."

"I know all about that," Jennifer said impatiently. "Ivy told me everything."

"So? Why did you go down the path?"

"Um . . . hold on," Jennifer said; then, muffling the phone, "Henry, baby, I'm going to take this call in that empty office, okay?" She came back on the line. "Wait a minute, Jane."

After a few moments Jennifer picked up again. "All right. When Ivy and I were having our cigarettes, Ivy told me that that sleazeburger, Larry Graham, had the hots for her and wanted her to meet him on the path at nine. I started teasing Ivy about it. Then, just as a goof, I ran over to the path to see if Larry was already there waiting for her. I did start down the path, but it was so dark I couldn't see three steps in front of me. I got creeped out and turned around and came back out of the woods. Any more questions?"

"No," Jane said, thanked her, and rang off.

It was almost time to go home. She tried to concentrate on the first draft of a manuscript she had recently received from Carol Freund, one of her biggest clients, but it was no use. She stared out her office window at the village green, dark gray and winter-gloomy. It had begun to snow, the flakes drifting toward her window and melting when they hit the glass.

Drifting . . . A conversation with Stanley came back to her, about the reception Adam and Rhoda had hosted, about people drifting in and out. Then she remembered passing Arliss's room and hearing her berating someone. Whom had Arliss been berating, and about what? It might be totally irrelevant . . . or it might not. She decided to call Arliss and ask her to lunch.

"Why, Jane?" Arliss asked with characteristic bluntness. "I just saw you last week."

"I know, but there's something I want to discuss with you."

"Go ahead."

"I'd prefer to do it in person."

Arliss let out an impatient groan. "Now you've got me all nervous, like you're going to tell me something bad about one of your clients I'm publishing." One client Jane had with Arliss was Carol Freund, whose manuscript sat before her on the heap.

"No, it's nothing like that. That much I can tell you."

"I see," Arliss said, though she clearly didn't. "Are you free tomorrow?"

"Absolutely," Jane replied, and they made arrangements.

The following morning, Jane stopped at the Shady Hills Police Station. Stanley was waiting for her in his office doorway. They stepped inside and briefly kissed.

"I've been thinking about our conversation yesterday afternoon," he said, dropping into the seat behind his desk as she sat down in his visitor's chair. "I shouldn't ask you this, because I already know the answer, but you never did stop playing detective, did you?"

"Nope. Haven't gotten much of anywhere, though," she added ruefully.

"Neither have we," he admitted. "Though one of the men I had searching the woods did find a flashlight Adam has identified as one he kept in the storage room. It was under a bush near the beginning of the path down to the pond."

"Interesting," she said. "Now. Do you want to know what I've learned?"

"You know I do."

"Good," she said, hunkering down, and carefully told him what she'd learned so far from all the people she'd talked to. It took a good half hour.

"That's a lot," he said when she was finished, his tone full of admiration.

"Thanks. Only problem is, any and all of them could have killed Ivy. Every single one had both motive and opportunity. The only ones in the clear are Adam and Rhoda and the people at their reception. Actually," she corrected herself, "the people at the reception aren't even in the clear. You told me everyone was drifting in and out."

"That's right." He grinned mischievously. "What if together the people at the reception planned Ivy's murder, one of them carried it out, and then they all covered for each other? Like that Agatha Christie novel."

"Stanley," Jane said in annoyance, "this is no joke."

"I'm not joking."

"Yes, you are, and it's not funny. This is my oldest friend we're talking about." She gazed dejectedly at her fingernails, which she realized she needed to have done. "I'm very frustrated —"

"Of course you are."

"— that you don't understand how important it is to me to discover the truth behind what happened to her. You're treating this like all your other cases." Tears came to her eyes.

"I'm sorry, Jane. I didn't mean it to sound that way. I do know how important she was to you."

She sniffed. "Apology accepted. Now where's the bag and the suitcase?"

"Oh, right. Just a minute." He left the office and returned a moment later with Ivy's red leather drawstring handbag and a large black suitcase on wheels. He handed the bag to Jane.

She opened it, peered inside, and rummaged about. Stanley had been right. She found nothing but everyday items like keys, chewing gum, cigarettes, a lighter, some makeup, a nail file, a purse containing a few bills and some change, a Visa card, an ATM card, Ivy's driver's license, and photos of Marlene and Jane. No notes, no paper, not even a small notepad.

She pulled the bag shut and placed it on Stanley's desk. "All right, how about the suitcase?"

He placed it on his desk and unzipped it. In it lay a messy assortment of clothes, more makeup, a pair of running shoes, a small blow-dryer, and, as Stanley had said, three issues of *The Enquirer.* Idly Jane lifted out the tabloids and regarded them. On the top copy, someone — presumably Ivy — had drawn a mustache on Cher. With a little laugh Jane flipped to the next newspaper. The headline read HOLLYWOOD STARS' INCOGNITO TRICK — NO MAKEUP! Below it was a quiz titled *Guess Who?* consisting of a row of women's unmade-up faces, labeled only A, B, C, and D. Beneath each picture Ivy had penciled in her guesses: Demi Moore, Kelly McGillis, Roseanne, Mary Tyler Moore.

"Ever the intellectual," Stanley quipped, and Jane shot him an icy look. Shaking her head, she placed the newspapers back into the suitcase.

"Wait, missed something," Stanley said, and pulled out the third tabloid, whose left margin was crammed with messy ballpoint doodles.

She glanced at them and shrugged. A

French poodle with exaggerated pom-pom fur. The word *Johnny,* written three or four times in different sizes. A snowman. A banana. Dollar signs. Two palm trees —

Jane pulled the paper closer.

"What is it?" Stanley asked.

"Nothing," she said, though unsure why. Ivy had drawn the same image four times: two palm trees, trunks crossed, with six coconuts at the base of their trunks.

"What?" he asked insistently. "Hieroglyphics?"

"Mm, that's it," she said, dropped the papers into the suitcase, and zipped it shut. "You're right," she said with a sad little smile. "Nothing here."

He zipped the suitcase shut. At the door of his office he gave her a kiss. "I'll call you later."

"Well, what is it?" Arliss said before her bottom had even settled in her chair. They were at Dig, Jane's least favorite restaurant.

"Take it easy," Jane said. "Why are you still wearing your coat?"

"I'm not," Arliss said, and shrugged it off, letting it fall onto the back of her chair.

"Why don't you check it?"

"I never check my coat. Why should I

pay somebody a dollar to hang up my coat and then take it off the hanger for me?"

"Wow. I guess publishing salaries are as bad as ever."

"Easy for you, Jane Stuart. Big-shot agent with hotsy-totsy clients. I'm a single woman — yes, making a not-gigantic salary — and I have to be careful."

Jane had never considered herself either a big shot or hotsy-totsy, but did not respond to this comment. Nor did she remind Arliss that she, too, was a single woman who had to be careful. Of one thing, however, she was reasonably certain: She earned more money than Arliss.

Arliss flipped the napkin off the bread basket and tore two thick slices off the French bread. She began slathering one of them with strawberry butter. "Even the way I eat," she went on in her annoying monotone. "I make lunch my big meal of the day so that Millennium can foot the bill."

"All right, Arliss," Jane said, rolling her eyes, "I get the point."

Arliss made an unattractive pouting expression with her mouth. "Fine. So," she said, meeting Jane's gaze, "what is it you couldn't discuss with me on the telephone?"

"It's about the retreat."

Arliss looked at her in frank surprise. "What about it? Did they find out who killed your friend?"

"No, that's not it. It's about something I heard you say."

"What?" Arliss threw down her slice of bread. "What did I say?"

The waiter arrived. "Would you like to hear our specials today?"

"No!" Arliss barked at him, and he turned and fled. "Now what's this all about, Jane? Stop pussyfooting around. What were you doing, eavesdropping on me or something?"

"Not intentionally. It was last Thursday night, after the group reading. I was heading down the corridor to my room when I passed your room and heard you, well, yelling at someone."

Arliss eyed Jane coldly. "What was I saying?"

"Now let me see if I can remember. It was something like, 'If you want to keep this working, you have to read them.' Then you called whoever it was you were talking to lazy and said something like, 'You should have told her you can't talk about them.' Who were you talking to? What were you talking about?"

Arliss looked at her as if she were crazy. "Why should I tell you that? What business is it of yours? What does it have to do with anything?"

"Now calm down. My guess is that it was Brad Franklin you were talking to, and that the 'her' you were referring to was Ivy. If I'm right, your conversation could have something to do with Ivy's murder."

Arliss pondered this, rubbing a few strands of her lank brown hair between her thumb and forefinger. At last she said, "You're right, it was Brad I was talking to. I remember it now. We were talking about his work as an instructor at the retreat. He was complaining to me that it was turning out to be more work than he'd expected and he didn't want to do it. I told him he had to read Red Pearson's work more carefully. You remember that Red was Brad's student."

"Yes, I remember," Jane said flatly, staring at Arliss. "What about when you said, 'You should have told her you can't talk about them'? Who were you referring to? Shouldn't have told *whom* about *what?*"

Arliss pursed her lips and shrugged.

Jane said, "Know what I think?"

"No, what?"

"That you're lying."

Arliss slammed her hand down on the

table, drawing the attention of the couples to either side. "How dare you call me a liar!"

"Knock it off, Arliss." Jane checked her watch. "I haven't got all day. Either you tell me the truth or I sic Detective Greenberg on you."

Arliss calmed down somewhat. "Supposing — just supposing — I'm not telling you the truth about what I was saying and who I was saying it to, what makes you think I was talking about Ivy?"

"Well, were you? You still haven't told me who 'her' was. If you were talking about Ivy, it's important. Everything Ivy did and said is important in this investigation. So . . . were you talking about Ivy?" Jane peered at her shrewdly. "Did it have anything to do with Ivy's saying Brad had a cushy setup?"

Arliss tossed her head from side to side. "Oh, all right — yes!"

"Okay," Jane said with a note of triumph, "now we're getting somewhere. Let's start again." But suddenly the truth came to her, like a light being switched on in her head. Her mouth fell open, and she stared at Arliss in wonder.

"What is it?" Arliss asked suspiciously.

"It's *you*."

"What's me?"

"*You* ghost all those celebrity novels, not Brad. I'm right, aren't I?"

Arliss's gaze dropped to her menu. "Yes," she said in a tiny, cracking voice. Jane wondered if she was about to cry.

"Why?" Jane asked.

Arliss looked up. "Because I love him!" she blurted out, again drawing stares from each side of the table.

"It makes perfect sense."

"Does it?" Arliss asked nastily. "Or are you going to start judging me? I can't openly be the ghostwriter on the celebrity books Millennium publishes, because I'm an editor there. It would be a conflict of interest. But I have the talent for it, Jane. So Brad and I worked out an arrangement. We've been doing it for years. He —"

"He's your front, your beard."

Arliss simply nodded. "After the group reading Thursday night, Brad came to my room. He was upset. He told me he and Ivy had been chatting, and he had accidentally revealed the name of one of the celebrities he ghosts for. As it happened, Ivy had read all of that celebrity's books. She got all excited and wanted to discuss them with Brad. But of course Brad couldn't discuss them, because not only does he not really write them, but he never even bothers to read what I write. *That's* what I was saying to him — that he can't be so lazy, he has to at least read the books if we're going to keep making this setup work. Then I asked him why he didn't simply tell Ivy he wasn't allowed to talk about the books he ghostwrites.

"Brad finally managed to change the subject, but he could tell that Ivy was suspicious." Arliss threw back her head defiantly. "So now you know our dirty secret. If you've got any decency, you'll *keep* it a secret."

"I will," Jane said sadly.

"Thank you, Jane," Arliss said, surprised. "May I ask why you would do that for us?"

"Because although what you're doing is not only immoral but also illegal, it's not my place to spill the beans. I feel sorry for you, Arliss. I only hope you're getting a big enough kickback from Brad that you're not really as poor as you make yourself out to be."

"I do all right. As for your pity, you can stuff it." Arliss closed her menu. The waiter returned. "We're not eating after all," she snapped at him. He scurried off, and Arliss started squirming into her coat.

"I'm not feeling very hungry either," Jane said, rising from her chair.

Arliss started away from the table, then stopped and turned to Jane. "So tell me. Was our conversation really something you needed to know about? Are you happy now?"

"I'm not happy, Arliss, but yes, it was definitely something I needed to know about."

Arliss narrowed her eyes. "How so?"

"Because it implicates both you and Brad as suspects in Ivy's murder. Ivy had figured out your scam, or was on the verge of doing so. You and Brad would have had a strong financial incentive to keep her quiet."

There was an odd silence. Jane and Arliss looked down to see that the couples at each side were watching them in fascination. "Mind your own business!" Arliss snapped at them, then turned on her heel and stomped from the restaurant.

Jane wasn't far behind.

Chapter Twenty-four

"You haven't touched your dinner, missus," Florence said, her face full of concern. "Did I overcook the meat?"

"No, Florence, it's delicious," Jane said. "I'm just thinking."

Nick turned to her, chewing on a piece of meat with his mouth wide open.

"No see food, please," Jane said absently.

Nick clamped his mouth shut. "What are you thinking about, Mom?"

"Ivy," she replied, her tone despondent.

"I'm done," he said. "May I please be excused?"

"Sure."

He ran off.

"Has Detective Greenberg made any progress?" Florence asked.

"Not really. It's not as if we don't know anything. We know a lot. In fact, the lodge was positively jumping the night Ivy was killed, and my guess is that we know about virtually all of it. And yet . . ."

"And yet, missus?" Florence paused, her fork in midair.

"And yet there's one thing that keeps troubling me."

"Yes?"

"Okay," Jane said. "You're smart. Let's see what you make of this. Ivy was going after a big story for the newspaper where she worked. A story so big that I don't think she would have risked leaving her notes in her apartment." She hadn't told Florence about Ivy's room having been searched. "She must have had notes, a few words, something. Where would she have put them?"

"That's easy," Florence said. "She would have kept them with her at all times. That's what I would do."

"I thought the same thing. But nothing was found on Ivy, in her room, or in her handbag or suitcase. Where else could these notes possibly be? It would have had to be someplace she knew was safe."

"Easy again," Florence said with a smile. "Right here."

Jane frowned at her. "Here?"

"Sure. In this house. She would have left the notes here and then picked them up after the retreat. Don't forget, Ivy didn't know she wasn't coming back here."

For a moment Jane stared at her. Then she slowly rose. "You know, I think you may have something. Excuse me."

She hurried out to the foyer, up the stairs, and along the hallway to the guest room. Her gaze went immediately to the nightstand to the left of the bed. Rushing over to it, she pulled open its one drawer and gazed down upon a small spiral-bound notebook. She flipped it open. On the first page were several notes:

hiding
corporate layers — have to pierce them
    to top
speak to club owner, manager — other
    employees
speak to neighbors
city records — public?

The second page, the only other page in the notebook that had been used, bore only a drawing:

"Find anything, missus?" Florence poked her head into the room.

Jane slipped the notebook into the pocket of her skirt and went out to the hallway. "Yes. You were right. Ivy did leave a notebook in the night table. But I'm afraid there's not much in it."

Florence looked disheartened.

"But thank you for the tip," Jane said, descending the stairs. "Now let's finish that delicious dinner you made."

Chapter Twenty-five

That evening, Jane sat in the laundry room, staring unseeing at Winky and the six kittens while Nick moved excitedly around the box, jotting in his notebook.

She was thinking again about Arliss and Brad. Were they really suspects? Would either or both of them have committed murder to protect this secret? People had been known to murder for far less, though Jane didn't feel it was likely in this case. And Arliss had confessed to her arrangement with Brad without putting up much of a fight; why would she have done so, if this was a secret worth killing for?

She remembered life with Ivy all those years before in the dorm at college. Ivy, always full of energy, eager to participate, but never really one of the crowd . . . a person people often laughed at behind her back.

Jane frowned at this memory. She recalled that sometimes she was aware that she was Ivy's friend simply because she pitied her.

A sad, unfair end to an empty, unfulfilled life. Would her murderer escape justice? Perhaps. Neither the police nor Jane had made any real, meaningful progress.

Vaguely she was aware that Nick was leaning into the nest box, busily doing something with his hands. Focusing on him, she rose a little in her chair to see what he was doing, and frowned. He appeared to be tying small lengths of ribbon around the kittens' fluffy middles. They squirmed and squealed in protest.

"Nick! What are you doing? Stop that."

He looked up at her, wide-eyed. "But I have to, Mom."

"Have to what?"

He straightened, lengths of colored ribbon in one hand. "I'm color-coding the kittens. It makes tracking easier."

She frowned. "Color-coding? Tracking? What are you talking about?"

He tapped his notebook. "I was looking over my notes last night, and I noticed that when the kittens nurse, some get more time than others. I'm sure Winky would want to know this, so I'm tying these different colored ribbons around the kittens so she can keep them all straight and give them equal time."

Jane laughed. "Oh, Nicholas. That's very considerate, but Winky doesn't need colored ribbons to keep her kittens straight."

As if in agreement, Winky looked up at Jane and let out a loud meow.

Florence strolled into the room, carrying a bottle of laundry detergent. "Your mother is correct, Master Nick," she said, placing the bottle in the cupboard above the clothes dryer. "Besides which," she added with a lighthearted laugh, "cats are color-blind. The ribbons will all look the same to Miss Winky."

Jane's eyes popped open and she checked the clock on the nightstand: 6:23. She hadn't slept all night, not really. Her mind was too full of clues, images, numbers, bits and pieces, all swirling maddeningly.

Numbers . . .

Colors . . .

She sat bolt upright in the bed, threw aside the covers, quickly showered and dressed.

By seven o'clock she was at her office. She called Stanley, who had just arrived at the police station.

"Don't you see?" she said. "This case has been all about the senses — and we've been blind. Meet me at Larry Graham's apartment. I hope we're not too late."

★ ★ ★

Entering the parking lot in front of Hillside Gardens, Jane scanned the cars for Stanley's cruiser but didn't see it.

She got out and ran up to Larry Graham's door. Raising her arm to knock, she realized that it was ajar. She knocked anyway, then rang the bell. There was no answer.

"Larry —" she called through the crack. Still nothing.

Something pressed against her leg and she jumped. Looking down, she saw a long furry nose. She pushed the door open and knelt to pat Alphonse, who responded with a high whimper.

She walked in past the dog, who didn't seem to want to move. The living room was empty.

"Larry —" she called again.

She went out the rear door of the living room, along a narrow corridor, and into the kitchen.

A hand roughly grabbed the left side of Jane's neck at the same time that something sharp and cold jabbed the right side. She gasped.

"Don't move, unless you want a screwdriver through that pretty neck."

She slid her gaze sideways to look at

Larry. On his colorless face was a look of fierce determination, as if he was afraid of doing this wrong. A drop of sweat ran from his upper lip into his mouth.

"I expected to find you dead," she said, not moving.

"Did you now? That's very interesting, since it's going to be the other way around." He tightened his grip on her neck, pushing the screwdriver harder against her.

"Ow."

"Shut up. Now here's what we're going to do. You're going to walk in front of me to my truck. It's parked right out- side. If you try anything funny, this screwdriver goes right into your back. You got it?"

"Yes. Where are we going?"

"For a ride. Go."

She walked toward the front door.

"Not that way. We're going out the back door."

Alphonse appeared in front of her and stuck his nose between her legs.

"Alphonse!" Graham shouted. "Go lie down."

With a whimper the dog retreated to the corner of the kitchen and fell onto his side, watching them with big sad brown eyes.

They reached the apartment's back door.

"Open it," Graham commanded, and she pulled it inward and started out.

"That's my truck over there," he said in a low voice right behind her, and pointed to a beat-up dark gray pickup parked to the right. "Let's go."

She considered making a break and running for it. Surely she was in better condition than he was. If she was going to do it, the time was now.

"Don't try running or anything," he said, as if reading her mind, and she felt the screwdriver jab hard into her coat, right in the middle of her back. "It would be so easy."

Her heart sank. She walked slowly to the passenger door of the pickup truck and he opened it. "Get in and roll down the window."

"What?"

"Just do it."

She got in. The truck's cab was littered with greasy hamburger wrappers, empty paper and Styrofoam cups, and yellow carbon copies of invoices headed LARRY GRAHAM, ELECTRICAL CONTRACTOR. The air in the cramped space had a stale, sweaty smell.

"Roll down the window," Graham said.

She'd forgotten. She rolled it down. As soon as she did, he reached in and unscrewed the pop-up-style door lock, removed it, and dropped it into his shirt pocket. In its place in the door was merely an empty hole.

"In case you decided to get adventurous," he said, and made his way around to the other side and got in. He started the truck, shifted it into gear, backed out, and started around the parking lot toward the exit.

"So you did kill Ivy," she said, turning to him with a look of loathing, as they left Hillside Gardens.

In response he picked up the screwdriver from where he had set it beside him on the seat and brandished the tool in the air. She saw now that it was huge, at least a foot long.

"Where are we going?"

"It doesn't matter." He laughed, his fat shoulders shaking. "You certainly won't care."

He turned onto Route 46, heading east.

In her bag, her cell phone rang.

He turned to her sharply. "Give it to me. *Don't answer it.*"

She found the phone in her bag and

297

handed it to Graham. He flipped it open and immediately terminated the call. Then he dialed a number. After a few moments he said, "We're on our way there. . . . Yeah, me and her. . . ." He snapped the phone shut and it immediately started to ring again. He rolled down his window and tossed the phone out. Jane heard it hit the pavement with a clatter, and the ringing abruptly stop. Had it been Stanley? she wondered. Florence or Nick? Daniel?

"Sorry, wrong number," he muttered.

"That was an expensive cell phone," she said quietly.

"You won't be needing it."

"Who did you just call?"

"None of your beeswax," he shouted. "Now sit back, relax." Suddenly he thought of something, and his face lit up. "Hey, my manuscript's in the backseat if you want to read it. I wrote some more."

"No, thanks, I'll pass."

He gave her a hateful look through slitted eyes. "You didn't really think my writing had promise, did you?"

"No."

"You were just, like, manipulating me to get me to talk?"

"Yes."

"Phony bitch."

"Murderer." She sat up in renewed anger. "Where are you taking me?" she demanded.

"None of your business," he snapped back. "Now keep your mouth shut. It's a long way and I don't think I can take much more of you. Pushy broad."

He switched on the radio and found the news. The police had captured the bus hijacker in a wooded section of Kinnelon, New Jersey, and identified him as Gary Larkin, twenty-nine, of Lyndhurst. Apparently he had been distraught after his wife left him and he lost his job in the same week.

Graham laughed a wheezing laugh. "See! I still can't believe your bubble-brained friend thought it was me."

Jane opened her mouth to protest.

His laughter died instantly. "I said keep your mouth shut, and I meant it." He turned up the radio.

Jane gazed out the window as the Willowbrook Mall swept by. She slid a glance at Graham and saw that he had moved the massive screwdriver to his lap. It occurred to her to grab the steering wheel and make him lose control of the truck, but what good would it do her? She couldn't throw open her door, because he had the lock in his shirt pocket. She considered grabbing for the screwdriver, using it on him, somehow getting the truck to stop. No, he was bigger and stronger than she was, and she would undoubtedly end up being the one impaled. She'd have to wait until they got wherever he was taking her to make her break.

He was heading for New York City. He had driven from Route 46 to Route 3, through the Meadowlands. Now they were on 495, stuck in the Lincoln Tunnel traffic at rush hour.

The truck was at a near standstill. If only she could get her door open . . . She glanced around at the surrounding cars. Could she somehow get the attention of another driver? No, everyone had his gaze fixed on the road, jockeying for that next inch forward.

As they approached the Lincoln Tunnel toll booths, she considered screaming to the toll collector. But at the last moment Larry veered into an E-ZPass lane and drove right through.

Emerging from the tunnel, Graham went west on 42nd Street and continued on it all the way to the West Side Highway, onto which he turned north.

"Where are we going?" she demanded again, glancing to the left across the Hudson River at New Jersey.

He ignored her. He remained on the West Side Highway for some time, finally getting off at West 96th Street. He took this east all the way to Park Avenue, onto which he turned left. They were in East Harlem, passing bodegas, tiny coffee shops and pizzerias, apartment buildings.

Abruptly he turned right onto East 116th Street, drove halfway down the block, and pulled into a space on the right side of the street beside a massive stone building.

Jane looked around. "You can't park here. There's a fire hydrant."

With a grunt of exasperation he held the screwdriver aloft. "Don't you ever shut up? Roll down your window."

She did, as he got out and came around the front of the truck toward her door. She considered scrambling to his side and bursting out his door, but in the next instant he was looking in at her through the window. Maybe she could make a run for it once she was on the sidewalk.

"Okay, here's what's gonna happen," he said in a low voice, though the street was deserted. He took her door lock from his shirt pocket and screwed it back into the hole. Then he pulled it up. "We're going into this building here."

She glanced up at it. "Why?"

"Because I said so. Don't you worry about it. Like I told you, pretty soon it won't matter."

So he would murder her, too. She saw that there was no escape now. She was going to die, just like Ivy. She thought of Nicholas and a great dread rose in her — dread of his losing his mother at ten years old, dread of not being around to watch him grow up, get married, have children.

She got out of the truck and walked ahead of him. Once again she felt the screwdriver press into her back.

She gazed up at the building. She knew what it was now. A car sped past them on the street, and was gone.

"In here," he said. "Stop."

She halted and peered into a small courtyard in the building's side. "Where?"

"Come on," he said impatiently, and gave her a sharp shove toward the building. Now she could see steps leading up to a door. "That's right, up there," he said, and when they had climbed the steps, he took a bunch of keys from his pocket, reached in front of her, unlocked the door, and pushed it open. Beyond it was a gloomy dimness. She could see a wall streaked with black. A smell suddenly reached her — a sour, acrid odor that made her gag. The smell of burning, of charred wood . . . and flesh.

"Oh," she said, holding her coat over her mouth.

"You get used to it," he said, and pushed her inside.

Graham produced a large flashlight that he must have brought from the truck and switched it on. They stood in a long corridor off which a number of doors opened on both sides. "Go to the end," he said, shoving the screwdriver at her back with his other hand. When she had reached the second-to-last door on the right, he said, "This door. Go."

She pushed it open and took a cautious step inside. Graham swept his flashlight slowly around a vast, cavernous room that had clearly been ravaged by fire. The walls and high ceiling were charred black. Cracks ran up and down and from side to side like alligator skin, indicating to Jane that the fire that had raged here had reached an extraordinarily high temperature.

Strewn among black pillars were the

charred remains of tables and chairs, merely blackened boards and sticks now. The center of the great room was oddly clear. A dance floor, Jane realized.

"Why have you brought me here?" she asked, though she knew.

He didn't answer, instead continued to sweep his flashlight around the immense room.

At that moment they heard rhythmic footsteps, the sound of a woman's high-heeled shoes. Graham fixed the beam on a doorway exactly opposite the one through which they had come. A woman stepped into the bright yellow circle of light and started toward them, strolling between the bits of burned furniture, her hands plunged deep in the pockets of a full-length fur coat the exact same blond color as her hair.

Chapter Twenty-six

Her scent reached Jane first — roses and violets, sickly sweet against the stench of rotting ashes. Then Tamara Henley stopped a few feet from Jane and Graham, looked Jane up and down, and smiled ruefully. "And to think I once wanted to have lunch with you."

"I can't make it," Jane said, her voice brimming with contempt.

Tamara threw back her head and laughed. "Oh, you definitely will not be able to make it." Her coat was of luscious beige chinchilla. Not a strand of her hair was out of place, and she was heavily made up. A small cascade of diamonds hung from each ear.

"All dressed up . . ." Jane said.

"And so many places to go. I've got another of our buildings to go to this morning, then a luncheon and board-of-directors meeting at the Frick. I certainly don't have time for your nonsense."

"*Nonsense?* You murdered my best friend."

Tamara shrugged indifferently. "She should have minded her own business."

"She was about to discover that you and your husband own this place. The Boriken Social Club, once St. Paul the Apostle Church."

"Now you see," Tamara broke in peevishly. "That was exactly the problem with your cheap little friend. She failed to make a very important distinction. Foss and I own this *building*. We *rented* it to the people who ran the Boriken Social Club. There's a world of difference."

Jane looked at her as if she were mad, which Jane realized she undoubtedly was. "No, there isn't. As the owners, you were responsible for meeting the building code, for installing a sprinkler system, making sure there were enough exits. Because of you and your husband, eighty-seven people died in this room."

"It wasn't our fault some lunatic decided to start a fire outside the exit to get back at his cheating girlfriend!" Tamara shouted.

"No, but it was your fault there was only one exit — that one. Those poor people had nowhere to go."

"Actually, there were two exits: the front door and the one you two just came through. Is it our fault that idiot started his fire in front of one of them? Besides, the club owner could have renovated at any time." Tamara shook her head impatiently. "We're going in circles, and I'm getting extremely bored." She turned to Graham. "Thank you for bringing her here."

Graham stood up a little straighter, as if Tamara were his general. "My pleasure, Tammy."

Tamara approached him and patted him on the back. He smiled and nodded modestly. As Jane watched, something popped out of his Adam's apple — the sharp tip of a thin metal rod. Graham's eyes bugged out, and he put his hands to his throat and turned and stared at Tamara. She raised one leg and with an elegant gold high-heeled pump gave him a firm kick in the side. He crashed to the floor, landing on his back. Blood spurted from his throat, getting on his hands, which now merely fluttered in the vicinity of his neck. As Jane watched in horror, his eyes grew glassy and lifeless.

Jane recoiled in horror.

"I told him not to call me that," Tamara said. She bent and grabbed the flashlight from where it had fallen beside him. Shining it on Graham's face, she watched him dispassionately for a moment. Then she bent again, roughly turned Graham's head to the side, and yanked out the ice pick she had used to kill him. Its tip shone reddish-black, as if it had been dipped in paint.

Straightening, Tamara noticed a large splotch of blood on her coat. "Oh, pooh!" she cried. "Look at my coat. And I've got my luncheon and board meeting."

Jane, heart banging, short of breath, regarded this monster, then looked down at Graham. "Why did you do that?" she asked, though she knew the answer.

"Oh, he deserved it," Tamara tossed off. "He tried to blackmail me. Me!"

Of course, Jane thought. And he'd gotten the idea from William Ives, who had blackmailed him. Jane said, "Graham knew you'd heard him and Ivy making plans to meet on the path. He knew you knew she would be there. Then he arrived at the pond and found her dead."

"Mm," Tamara said, regarding the ice pick thoughtfully.

Jane continued, "While Larry and Ivy were talking in the lounge, he heard you in the conference room. He hurried out to see who might have overheard them, but you were gone. But he did smell your distinctive perfume." She thought back. "That's what he meant when he made an

308

odd comment to me about there being some trails you couldn't see. *Scent.*"

Tamara's mouth dropped open, and she glared in annoyance at the corpse of Larry Graham. "*That's* how he knew I'd been there? Ooh, that stinking liar. He told me he'd seen me. I *do* have to stop wearing so much scent."

"The point is, he must later have put two and two together. He knew you had known Ivy would be on that path. He knew *he* hadn't killed Ivy. So he took a flyer, blackmailed you, and hit the jackpot. What did he want?"

Tamara laughed. "Work!"

"Work?"

"Yes, he knew Foss was a developer. Graham wanted the job doing the electrical work in our next building. I told him he could have it, with a few conditions. First, that he go to Ivy's office and get hold of any files she had on her 'big story.' He found nothing. So I told him to get into Ivy's apartment and look there. Nothing again. I figured she must have had her notes with her, but I couldn't very well search her room at the lodge — the police would have taken anything they'd found anyway — and I couldn't get into the po-lice station to search her luggage. I could only pray that nothing had been found.

"Then," Tamara went on, glancing at Graham's body, "last Saturday night, he called me. He said you'd been to see him twice asking questions, that you'd found out a lot. I had to find out how much you knew. Why do you think I invited you to my New Year's party — because I *like* you?" She shuddered. "I had to invite all those other dreadful people from the retreat to sort of — camouflage you, if you know what I mean. At my party, you said you'd made progress in finding Ivy's murderer. Well, I couldn't have that, could I? So this was my last condition for Mr. Graham — to bring you here."

And I walked right into your hands, Jane thought.

Tamara gazed down again at Graham's lifeless form and shook her head. "He wanted us to have an ongoing 'relationship,'" she said distastefully. "Can you imagine? He said he was 'growing' his business, that all he wanted to keep quiet was one big job a year."

Jane looked around, took in the charred surroundings. "I take it this was the next building."

"Not precisely. Our next building will be the one we'll build here after we tear this one down. That moron who started the fire outside the club had no idea what a favor he was doing us. Foss and I will collect the insurance and put up a magnificent fifty-story office building on this site — this *historic* site, I should say."

"An office building?"

"Absolutely," Tamara replied, regarding Jane as if she were intellectually deficient. "Harlem is hot now; don't you know that? The second Harlem renaissance. We have an ex-president here. Commercial rents are doubling. On 125th Street they're tripling. We'll have this building rented well before it's finished." She looked around in disgust. "But first we have to tear down this mess. Little will anyone know that you and your friend here will be in the rubble. I'll burn your bodies first, of course. I'll do that before I leave here this morning. I've brought some gasoline." With her free hand she vaguely indicated the dimness behind her.

She frowned. "I've got one question for you, Jane. Had you yet figured out that it was I who killed Ivy?"

"Yes."

"May I ask how? Was it my perfume?"

"Scent? No. It was color."

Tamara frowned. "Color?"

"You made a mistake about Ivy's sweater."

Tamara eyed Jane shrewdly. "What mistake?"

"The key to solving this case," Jane said thoughtfully, "was a comment made by my son's nanny, Florence, about cats being color-blind. Suddenly several details I'd ignored became extremely important — and made sense of everything."

"So," Tamara said petulantly, "cats are color-blind. Big deal. What does that have to do with anything?"

"So are you." Tamara made no response, just watched Jane, who went on, "That's why your clothes sometimes clash. That's why you said both of the wreaths in your room at the lodge were the same color. People with color blindness can't tell the difference between red and green.

"In the conference room, when you were talking about the wreaths, I saw Adam frown. But he didn't frown because you'd said they were tacky and offended him. He frowned because you'd said they were both the same color. He knew they weren't and was puzzled by your remark."

Jane's eyes unfocused as she cast her thoughts back to the night Ivy died. "Red and green . . . Ivy was wearing a red sweater on the night she died. You said the last time you'd seen Ivy was in the lounge, and that she was brushing snow from her green sweater. But when Ivy came into the lounge, she was still wearing the white fisherman's knit sweater Jennifer had lent her.

"In truth, when you last saw Ivy — on the path, by the light of the flashlight you'd stolen from the lodge's storage room — she had already given the sweater back to Jennifer. Ivy's own sweater was red, but you remembered it as green because you can't tell the difference between the two colors. But it didn't matter whether you remembered the sweater as red or green. What mattered was that you didn't remember it as white, and thereby gave yourself away."

Tamara shook her golden-coiffed head in amazement. "You are a marvel." Then her face grew pensive. "I wonder if I'll need to take care of Adam. If he 'puts two and two together,' as you put it . . ."

"Monster," Jane spat. "Cold-blooded murderer. You stole the ice pick from the kitchen at the lodge, went down the path, and waited for Ivy, who planned to meet Larry, who she must have believed was the bus hijacker." She shook her head sadly.

313

"She thought she was blackmailing him. He thought she was into some kind of kinky foreplay.

"So what did you do when Ivy got to the end of the path? Talk to her a little? Just jump out and stab her?"

"Does it matter? Yes, we talked a little. I pretended I'd come out for some fresh air. I got her onto the subject of the story she was pursuing about the Boriken Social Club. She told me she'd discovered that the company that owned this building was Coconut Grove Development. The irony was, she hadn't the slightest idea Coconut Grove was Foss and me."

"But you knew it was only a matter of time before she discovered that . . . before she pierced the many corporate layers you and your husband had placed between you and your tenants to protect yourselves, to keep you anonymous. Ivy's story would have ruined you both, would have put you in jail for a very long time. How did you know she was working on that story?"

"She simply started bragging about it the first night we were at the lodge. That shriveled little old man, William, and I were sitting in the conference room, having some fruit we'd scrounged up in the kitchen. Ivy came in and began chattering

314

about her 'big story' behind the Boriken Social Club fire, about how the company that owned the building would be in major trouble when she was through. Not to mention the big promotion she'd get at *Skyline*."

Tamara looked irritated. "I kept trying to press her for more details, to find out how much she knew. But then she changed the subject, and all she wanted to talk about was her daughter who died." She shrugged. "It didn't matter. I knew enough."

Jane gave an ironic laugh. "Ivy thought you didn't want to hear about Marlene because you were cold and unfeeling."

"I *didn't* want to hear about Marlene. Who cares about her foolish daughter?"

Jane ignored this last remark. "I found palm trees and coconuts on Ivy's desk blotter in her office at *Skyline* and elsewhere among her things. The palm and coconuts are, of course, your company's logo. The name *Tamara* means 'palm.' *Foss* is short for 'Forrest.' A palm forest . . ."

"Is a coconut grove," Tamara finished, looking endlessly bored.

"And in the center of the logo, of course, is a six, quite prominent. And at the bottom, *six* coconuts. Six, your lucky number. Very clever, really."

"No, you're very clever, Jane. You must be a whiz at *The New York Times* crossword puzzle."

Jane said, "At dinner the night Ivy was killed, when she said she had a story that would put someone in jail for years, we all naturally assumed she was talking about Johnny. But she was actually referring to whoever owned Coconut Grove Development.

"You and your husband are slumlords of the worst kind." Jane's voice was full of contempt. "You let this magnificent building — St. Paul the Apostle Church — become a firetrap. Yes, Ivy would have had one hell of a story. About your neglect that turned this place into a death box. About its lack of a sprinkler system, its inadequate exits. Your blatant building-code violations led to eighty-seven people getting trampled to death in a panicked stampede or dying from smoke asphyxiation." She looked around her, almost expecting the ghosts of those poor souls to appear, their screams to resound in the dimness.

"I told you," Tamara said through clenched teeth, "this club was owned by our *tenants*. Foss and I had nothing to do with it."

"You and your husband still feel no responsibility for what you've done — or not done," Jane marveled. "Slumlords rarely do. The way you look at it, you and Foss are the victims, am I correct?"

"Yes, for once you are."

Jane nodded. "You made this attitude quite clear when you said the owner of the house across the street from yours would be blamed for the negligence of his tenants. And when you scoffed when Red Pearson read from his novel based on the club fire: It wasn't to get back at him for criticizing your story; it was because his telling of the club fire tragedy was, to your way of thinking, inaccurate.

"Everyone had it wrong, you thought. Everyone was making you and your husband the culprits. So — in order to protect yourselves — you killed the woman who would make it all public."

"You bet I did," Tamara said resentfully. "I wasn't going to let some tacky little slut playing Lois Lane ruin everything Foss and I have built. Cause some huge scandal, turn Foss and me into another Harry and Leona Helmsley. No, thank you."

Tamara turned down the corners of her mouth disdainfully. "Ivy was an idiot. She started telling me this slob" — she gestured toward Graham's corpse — "was once a figure skater. She said Larry was going to skate for her, and turned around to look at the pond. That's when I stabbed her. She made the funniest little squeaking sound." She giggled.

Jane winced.

"It was quite easy, really," Tamara said. "Killing her, I mean." She held up the ice pick, admiring it. "I liked it so much that as soon as I'd decided I was going to get rid of you, I drove over to Fortunoff in Wayne and picked this up." She smiled. "Fortunoff. The Source."

She checked her slimly elegant watch. "Oh, dear, getting late. You've wasted enough of my time." Suddenly she lunged forward, like a fencer, thrusting the pick at Jane, jabbing her right hand. Hot pain seared the center of Jane's palm. She looked quickly and saw blood seeping from the wound.

She had no sooner looked up again than Tamara rushed forward with a cry, throwing her whole weight at Jane. Jane managed to grab the arm holding the pick and put all her strength into forcing it away. Tamara was surprisingly strong. For a moment, as they pushed at each other, their faces were only inches apart, and Jane

318

saw unadulterated hatred — and madness — in the other woman's eyes.

Jane drew back her right foot and kicked Tamara as hard as she could in the shin. Tamara let out a grunt of pain, the flashlight went flying from her hand, yet the pressure of her arm against Jane's barely lessened, and her hand still clutched the ice pick, its bloody tip now only inches from Jane's face.

With a great mustering of strength, Jane surged forward, and the two women toppled to the floor, Jane on top. The ice pick's handle hit the floor and was knocked out of Tamara's hand, landing a few inches from Larry Graham's inert body. Jane scrambled for it, grabbed it, and swiftly stood. Tamara had also gotten up and stood a few yards away, watching.

Jane clutched the handle of the ice pick with both hands, pointing its tip straight out before her. She waited. Tamara took a step closer.

"Stay back," Jane warned, but Tamara took another step. Jane broke out in a sweat, wondering if she could stab someone — even Tamara — even if it was to save her own life. Then a great rage overtook her and she realized that of course she could — could and would.

Tamara's foot came flying toward Jane, knocking the ice pick out of her hands. Tamara quickly retrieved it. Jane turned and ran.

She went back out the door through which she and Larry had come, and to the left down the long corridor. She ducked into one of the rooms toward the end on the left, unsure if Tamara had seen her.

Silently she slid behind the door, then stood as still as a statue, waiting, peering into the gloom through the crack of the door, between its hinges.

There was absolute quiet . . . then a crunch, followed by the faint creak of a floorboard not far away. Jane held her breath. She realized her hands were shaking.

And in the next instant Tamara was there, looking straight at her through the crack of the door. With all her might, Jane slammed the door into Tamara's face.

Tamara made an odd choking-gurgling sound, then collapsed.

Slowly Jane walked around the door. Tamara lay in a chinchilla sprawl, on her back, the ice pick having pierced her throat and emerged from the back of her neck. Her eyes were open, still full of gleaming hatred.

Jane gasped, turning quickly away.

Then Tamara moved and Jane returned her gaze to her in horror. Tamara's lips were moving. Cautiously Jane leaned over her, straining to make out what she was trying to say.

"Not . . . our fault," Tamara whispered. In a flash her hand flew up and grabbed Jane's face. Jane drew back, pulling at Tamara's arm, but couldn't loosen the clawlike grip, the fingernails digging into her cheeks.

And then, in the next moment, the grip was released as Tamara's hand went limp and her arm fell to her side.

Jane began to cry. Stepping over Tamara's body, she walked slowly down the corridor and found the door to the courtyard. There was Graham's pickup at the curb. She made her way toward it. As she reached it, her legs suddenly weakened and she faltered, grabbing at the truck for support.

"Lady, you okay?"

She looked up. A petite young woman came toward her wheeling a wire shopping basket full of groceries.

"I'm fine, thank you," Jane said, but her legs betrayed her again and she fell to the sidewalk.

The young woman rushed to her and helped her gently lie down.

"Help! Somebody help me!" Jane heard the woman cry.

"What's the problem?" came a young man's voice.

"I don't know what's the matter with her. Maybe drunk."

Through partially closed eyes Jane saw the young man's dark face — shrewd, serious — come near hers. "Lady," he said softly, "you okay?" Then she felt him touch her coat.

"Look at this," she heard him say.

"Oh, Lord. What is that?"

"What do you think it is? It's blood."

"Blood? Whose? Hers?"

"Hell, I don't know. Get a cop."

Chapter Twenty-seven

That afternoon, Jane sat at her favorite table at Whipped Cream, staring into a magnificent fire in the brick hearth. Stanley sat beside her, gently holding her bandaged right hand.

"Ivy, my poor old friend, was a tragic figure, really," Jane said. "She had poor judgment and was of weak moral character — she tried to blackmail Larry Graham, though for something he hadn't done — yet in the end she was killed because, for once in her life, she was trying to do something good — expose a terrible evil." Tears rolled down her cheeks.

Ginny, who had been behind the counter preparing hot cocoa for the three of them, appeared carrying a tray holding the three mugs. She, too, was crying. She set down the mugs on the table, then sat down beside Jane and took her other hand. Stanley put his arm around Jane's shoulders, and they all gazed at the holiday decorations surrounding the fireplace. Brilliant lights, like the ones in the café's window. Red and green . . .

"It's not fair," Jane said.

"No," Stanley agreed, "it's not fair." He gave her arm a soft, comforting squeeze. "Not fair at all."

"And so you see," Jane finished, smiling across the dinner table at Nick and Florence, "your comment, Florence, about cats being color-blind was the key to solving this case."

Nick, to whom Jane had finally revealed the truth about Ivy's death, sat very still, his gaze lowered to the table.

"A wreath of poinsettias and cranberries," Florence said thoughtfully. "You know, missus, at home in Trinidad, our national flower is the wild poinsettia — the chaconia."

Jane and Nick looked at her. She went on, "It is a very beautiful, deep-red flower and grows in the forests. To the people of Trinidad and Tobago, it represents the imperishability of life."

She shook her head, remembering, eyes unfocusing. "When I was a little girl of nine, my older brother Charles died. It was a terrible time. As the months passed, everyone in my family seemed to get back to normal except me. I could not rid myself of my deep sadness. One day my mother took me by the hand to our kitchen. On the table, in a vase, she had placed a glorious long spray of chaconia. It was early September, when this flower starts to bloom. It was so very red and lovely.

" 'Florence,' my mother said to me, 'look at the flower and think of Charles. And whenever you think of Charles, think of the flower and remember, he is still with us. In our hearts, he is still with us. He never went away.' "

"That's sad, Flo," Nick said, gazing solemnly across the table at her.

"No, Master Nicholas," Florence said with a laugh, "it is happy! Our friends never leave us, even when we cannot see them. What's important," she said, looking at Jane, "is that while our friends are still here on earth, we do our best to be kind to them. To be a good friend."

She gave Jane a reassuring nod.

"Thank you, Florence," Jane said softly.

"For what?" Nick asked.

Winky leapt onto the table with a joyous rumbling cry.

"Hey, Wink!" Nick cried happily. "You haven't done that in weeks." He turned to Florence. "I guess she knows life goes on, huh? That even though most of her babies are going away and she'll never see them again, she'll still have them, like you said."

"Yes, Master Nick," Florence said, gently removing Winky from the table. "She knows."

Author's Note

I hope you enjoyed reading *Icing Ivy*, my fourth Jane Stuart and Winky mystery. By now Jane, Nicholas, Florence, Stanley, Daniel, and all the other residents of Shady Hills are family to me, as I hope they are to you.

One of the reasons this book was such fun to write was that Winky became a mother, an event long in the planning. Though Jane, Nick, and Florence made it their business to find good homes for all of Winky's kittens, this is not always the case.

The Best Thing You Can Do for Your Cat

The fact is, there are too many kittens and too few good homes. Animal shelters are overburdened with unwanted animals. Each day tens of thousands of cats are born in the United States alone. At this rate, there are not enough homes for these animals, and millions of healthy cats and kittens are euthanized. Others are abandoned to fend for themselves against automobiles, cruel humans, the elements, and other animals.

Please spay or neuter your cat. Not only will you be stopping this unnecessary suffering, but you will also be doing something good for you and your pet.

Spayed and neutered cats are better, more affectionate companions because they focus their attention on their human families. They are less likely to bite. Unaltered cats often show more behavior and temperament problems than cats that have been spayed or neutered.

Spayed and neutered cats live longer, healthier lives.

Spaying a female eliminates its heat cycle; females in heat often cry incessantly, urinate frequently (sometimes all over the house), exhibit nervous behavior, and attract unwanted male cats. Spaying females eliminates the chance of uterine or ovarian cancer, and significantly reduces the likelihood of breast cancer and of a disease called pyometra.

Neutered males are less likely to spray and mark territory, and to roam in search of a mate, risking injury in traffic and fights with other males. Neutering males reduces the incidence of hernias, perianal tumors, and prostate disease, and eliminates the possibility of testicular cancer.

If you have reservations about spaying or neutering your cat, it may be because you believe one or more of the myths surrounding this practice. Spaying or neutering will not change your cat's personality. Nor will it make your cat fat and lazy — only a poor diet and lack of exercise will do that. Spaying and neutering are neither dangerous nor painful. These low-cost procedures are the most common surgeries performed on cats. With a minimal amount of home care, your pet will resume normal behavior in a few days.

If your cat gives birth, don't wait too long to have her spayed. Wait until two weeks after her kittens start to be weaned — in other words, six to eight weeks after she gives birth. Remember that a surgery appointment may need to be made several weeks ahead.

Remember also that kittens don't need to wait too long to be spayed or neutered. Veterinary societies and shelters have accepted early sterilization as safe. It can be done on cats as young as eight weeks old.

For more information, visit the Web site of The American Society for the Prevention of Cruelty to Animals at http://www.aspca.org.

Some of the best history is what we don't learn in school. When Jane learns that her friend Ivy has been stabbed with an ice pick, she says, "Like Trotsky . . ." and faints. What's the story behind that?

In 1940, the exiled Bolshevik leader Leon Trotsky was living in Mexico City. His greatest enemy, Joseph Stalin, had pursued him across continents via his murderous agents in an effort to assassinate him, but had thus far been unsuccessful.

Ultimately Trotsky's murder would be accomplished by a man named Ramon Mercader. Though Trotsky was protected by bodyguards, Mercader penetrated his defenses by means of a clever ruse. After ingratiating himself with the members of Trotsky's household and gaining their trust and acceptance, he arranged to meet personally with Trotsky on the pretext of discussing an article he had written. They did meet, and Trotsky dismissed the article as banal and without interest.

On the morning of August 20, Mercader showed up at Trotsky's villa and was again allowed to visit with Trotsky alone to discuss the article Mercader had written. Trotsky's wife, Natalia Sedova, later related: "I was in the room next door. There was a terrible piercing cry . . . Lev Davidovich [Trotsky's birth name] appeared, leaning against the door frame. His face was covered with blood, his blue eyes glistening without spectacles and his arms hung limply by his side. . . ."

Mercader had struck Trotsky in the back of the head with an ice pick he had hidden in the pocket of his khaki raincoat. According to Mercader himself, "I put my raincoat on the table so that I could take out the *piolet* [ice pick] in the pocket. When Trotsky started to read my article, I took the ax and, closing my eyes, gave him a tremendous blow on the head. The man screamed in a way that I will never forget — Aaaaaa! . . . very long, infinitely long. He got up like a madman, threw himself at me, and bit my hand — look, you can still see the marks of his teeth. Then I pushed him, so that he fell to the floor."

Trotsky's bodyguards rushed into the room and began to beat Mercader, who, having never killed before, was stunned at the sight of Trotsky on the floor. The guards wanted to kill Mercader on the spot, but Trotsky intervened: "He must be forced to talk."

Trotsky was rushed to the hospital. "The

doctor declared that the injury was not very serious," Natalia said. "Lev Davidovich listened to him without emotion, as one would a conventional message of comfort. Pointing to his heart, he said, 'I feel . . . here . . . that this is the end . . . this time . . . they've succeeded.' "

He underwent surgery and survived more than a day. He died 26 hours after being attacked, on August 22, 1940.

On some points of this legendary story, people disagree. Some say it was an ice *ax*, not an ice pick.

I immediately found this story fascinating. What mystery writer wouldn't? For my purposes in icing poor Ivy, an ice pick worked best.

Wheresoever You May Wander . . .

Curious about Florence's Curried Cascadura? The cascadura fish — or cascadoo, as it is commonly called — is about as Trinidadian a creature as one could find. This small, primeval fish from the Silurian age, with a scaly, armor-plated shell resembling that of the catfish, lives embedded in the freshwater mudflats of Trinidad's southern coast, as well as in sluggish rivers, ponds, and swamps.

Though this strange fish is served in Caribbean restaurants around the world, most of us do not have access to this delicacy. The following recipe, therefore, substitutes snapper for cascadura.

If you *are* fortunate enough to have real cascadura, remember that it must be washed thoroughly and meticulously in fresh water until all the mud on the fish is removed.

Florence's Curried "Cascadoo"

4 Servings

1 large shallot, finely chopped
1 piece of fresh thyme, finely chopped
1 piece of fresh parsley, finely chopped
1 leaf cilantro, finely chopped
½ teaspoon vinegar
¼ teaspoon salt
¼ teaspoon pepper
4 fresh snapper (or cascadura) fillets
¼ cup (60 milliliters) lime juice
1 tablespoon vegetable oil
1 large onion, chopped
3 tomatoes, chopped
3 cloves garlic, chopped
2 tablespoons curry paste
1 cup (250 milliliters) coconut milk

1 whole hot pepper wrapped in cheese-cloth and tied securely

Combine shallot, thyme, parsley, and cilantro in a cup with vinegar. Add salt and pepper. Marinate 4 snapper fillets in herb seasoning and lime juice for at least 2 hours.

Heat oil in a large pot. Add onion, tomatoes, and garlic and sauté for 2 minutes. Add curry paste and cook for another minute. Add coconut milk and simmer for 5 minutes. Add the marinated fish fillets and coat thoroughly with the curry sauce. Add the pepper, cover, and simmer until fillets are flaky — about 10 to 15 minutes.

Remove fillets and serve on a platter covered with the curry sauce. Serve with rice and vegetables.

From Havana With Love

Intrigued by the drink after which Jennifer Castaneda named her novel? I was. The *Mojito* (pronounced "moe-HEE-toe"), born in Cuba in the 1910s, is a refreshing rum drink popularized by the patrons of Havana's most famous bar, La Bodeguita del Medio — most notably Er-nest Hemingway. It's currently making a big comeback. Great with barbecue. Come to think of it, a *Mojito* would be a nice accompaniment to Florence's Curried Cascadura. Here's how to make one just the way "Papa" liked them. *¡Salud!*

Mojito Cocktail

½ teaspoon sugar
½ lime, juiced
1 sprig fresh mint, crushed
½ cup crushed ice (use ice pick? never mind)
2 fluid ounces (60 milliliters) light dry rum
4 fluid ounces (120 milliliters) soda water
1 sprig fresh mint for garnish

In a highball glass, stir together the sugar and lime juice. Bruise the mint leaves and drop them into the glass. Fill glass with crushed ice and pour in rum. Pour in soda water to fill the glass. Garnish with a sprig of mint.

I love hearing from readers. If you have a comment about *Icing Ivy* or any of my books, I invite you to e-mail me at evanmarshall@TheNovelist.com, or write to me at Six Tristam Place, Pine Brook, NJ 07058-9445. I always respond to reader mail. For a free bookmark, please send a self-addressed stamped envelope. Please visit my Web site at http://www.TheNovelist.com.

Evan Marshall

Like his sleuth Jane Stuart, EVAN MARSHALL heads his own literary agency. A former book editor, he has contributed articles on writing and publishing to numerous magazines and is the author of *Eye Language, The Marshall Plan for Novel Writing, The Marshall Plan Workbook*, and the Jane Stuart series, *Missing Marlene, Hanging Hannah*, and *Stabbing Stephanie*. He lives and works in Pine Brook, New Jersey, where he is at work on the next Jane Stuart and Winky mystery. You can e-mail him at: evanmarshall@thenovelist.com.